Roy Lancaster

Romeo and Juliet
&
The Merchant of
Venice

Limited Special Edition. No. 3 of 25 Paperbacks

Roy Lancaster was born in London and qualified as an architect, designing many projects throughout the Middle East, where he opened an office and spent most of his architectural working life. After retirement, he took up writing, mainly children's material. He now lives in Cheltenham with his wife.

For all children

Roy Lancaster

ROMEO AND JULIET
&
THE MERCHANT OF VENICE

AUSTIN MACAULEY PUBLISHERS™

LONDON • CAMBRIDGE • NEW YORK • SHARJAH

A CIP catalogue record for this title is available from the British Library.

ISBN 9781528950947 (Paperback)
ISBN 9781528972895 (ePub e-book)

www.austinmacauley.com

First Published (2020)
Austin Macauley Publishers Ltd
25 Canada Square
Canary Wharf
London
E14 5LQ

Romeo and Juliet

Romeo and Juliet was first performed in the mid-1590s; since then it has been the most popular and most performed of all Shakespeare's works. Its appeal probably lies in the fact that it touches on a number of social and emotional problems prevalent in the past and indeed in current times, in particular the machismo and derogatory attitude of men towards women and women's submissiveness. The core of the play is a bitter, continuous feud between two families, into which Shakespeare adds an explosive situation by introducing two young lovers, one from each of the feuding families. Their love is forbidden but they are ultimately united, in a sad and tragic way.

Characters in the Play

ROMEO

MONTAGUE	his father
LADY MONTAGUE	his mother
BENVOLIO	their kinsman
ABRAM	a Montague serving man
BALTHASAR	Romeo's serving man

JULIET

CAPULET	her father
LADY CAPULET	her mother
NURSE	to Juliet
TYBALT	kinsman to the Capulets
PETRUCIDO	Tybalt's companion
CAPULET'S COUSIN	
SAMPSON	
GREGORY	
PETER	serving men
ESCALUS	Prince of Verona
PARIS	the Prince's companion and Juliet's suitor
MERCUTIO	the Prince's kinsman and friend of Romeo

PARIS'S PAGE
FRIAR LAWRENCE
FRIAR JOHN
APOTHECARY
Three or four Citizens
Three Musicians
Three Watchmen
Attendants, Maskers, Torchbearers, a Boy with a drum, Gentlemen, Gentlewomen, Tybalt's Page, Serving men.

Act 1
Scene 1

Enter Sampson and Gregory armed with swords and shields. They talk of their feud with the Capulets. Gregory speaks.

"On my word we'll not be humbled, and hang our heads in shame,
Our necks will never fill a noose; we'll fight for our good name."
"I'd quickly act," said Sampson, "'gainst those, I so dislike,
A dog from their house would move me, to stand and draw and strike!"

"Montague men I'd push away, from the safety of the wall,
I'd replace them with their women, whose heads would start, to fall.
Ay! Their heads...or 'haps...their maidenheads, I could not care the less, they'll feel me though! for 'tis well known, I'm a pretty piece of flesh!"

"Be glad you are flesh," Gregory laughed, "for had you been a fish,
You'd have been a salty poor John, unfit to grace a dish.
But wait my friend and draw your sword, for trouble greets my eye,
Be on your guard, prepare to stand, a Montague comes by."

Enter Abrams with another serving man. Sampson whispers to Gregory.

"My sword is drawn, I'll guard your back, our name they'll not deride,
But let them be the first to strike, that the law is on our side."
"I'll frown as they pass," said Gregory, "with scorn upon my face,
Whilst you bite your thumb to goad them, into action...or disgrace."

Sampson bites his thumb, causing Abrams to speak to him.

"Do you bite your thumb at us sir?" Replied Sampson, "I do not,
But I do bite my thumb, yes indeed sir, do you quarrel sir or what?"
I've no need to quarrel," Abrams bragged, "I'm from a better house."
"You lie," roared Sampson, "ours is best, draw you Montague louse!"

They start to fight. Enter Benvolio, also drawing his sword. He tries to stop them as Tybalt follows in.

"Part you fools," cried Benvolio, "you know not what you do,
Pray help me Tybalt stop this fight, or our feuding will renew!"
"What!" cried Tybalt, "you'd talk peace, with a sword held in your hand,
I hate that word, as I hate you, prepare for your last stand!"

They fight. A crowd of citizens enter armed with clubs, knives and other weapons and start to attack the feuding families. As they do, they shout.

"Veronians, use your clubs and staves, come beat these creatures down,
The Capulets and Montagues, who sully our fair town.
We're so weary of their feuding, the deaths that each day greets,

Beat them down, don't let them spill more blood upon our streets."

Enter Old Capulet with his wife, a little later comes Old Montague and wife. Old Capulet speaks.

"What noise is this? Give me my sword, here's Montague my foe,
His blade is drawn so give me mine," his wife said firmly "NO!"
"You villain sir," cried Montague, "wife...don't hold me back."
"I'll not let you stir a foot!" she cried, "another man to hack!"

Enter Prince Escalus and attendants. He loudly calls to everyone.

"Rebellious subjects, foes of peace, who turn our fair town red,
Beasts who only quench your rage, when veins are fully bled.
On pain of torture drop your swords from those vile and bloody hands,
Hear the sentence I pass on you, for fouling these our lands."

"Old Capulet, Old Montague, our streets you have disturbed,
Your brawls have left our citizens, angry and perturbed.
Should you ever break our peace again, you'll forfeit with your life,
We'll no longer truck your ancient row, or tolerate the strife."
"YOU! Capulet, come with me now, to the common judgement place,
To hear and learn what else it is, that you may have to face.
And Montague, come after noon, your turn will then come due,
Now all depart for the judgement place, for further case review."

All depart except old Montague, who speaks to Benvolio

"Who was it who renewed the grudge? speak nephew, tell me who."
Benvolio answered, "'twas our staff, and that of their house too
I tried to part them, called for help, when the fiery Tybalt came,
But he attacked me, I'd no choice, but to fight him for our name."

"My Romeo was not involved," Lady Montague said,
But where is he, have you seen him? Not knowing fuels my dread."
Benvolio answered, "Madam, today at early mom,
I walked abroad to clear my mind, with the freshness of the dawn."

"I saw your son within the woods, towards him I did stride,
He soon became aware of me, and turned deeper in…to hide."
"Many a mom," said Montague, "he's been witnessed walking there,
His eyes hold tears to match the dew, his poor sighs cloud the air."

"But as soon as the sun arises, and overpowers night,
My son steals home to his darkened room, all windows shuttered tight.
His humour's black and soulful, portending something bad,
I pray good counsel can improve his mood that is so sad."

"Dear uncle," asked Benvolio, "have you learned what caused his pain?"
"No I have not," said his uncle, "friends too have tried…in vain."
Benvolio whispered, "Now he comes, pray uncle, stand aside,
I'll learn what is his grievance, I will not be denied."

Lady and Old Montague exit. Romeo enters and Benvolio greets him.

"Good morrow cousin, greetings," asked Romeo... "is it morn?"
Oh how my hours seem sad and long, each minute so forlorn."
"What sadness is it," Benvolio asked, "that makes hours long and fraught?"
"I do not have," said Romeo, "that, which makes them short!"

"I'm favoured not by the one I love, so my love is muffled still,
Love's true pathway lies unseen, such a sour and bitter pill.
Normality is chaos, what once was white...is black,
Feathers are lead and fire is cold, clear reasoning... I lack."

"But you do not laugh dear cousin, is what I've told too deep?"
"I do not laugh," Benvolio sighed, "because 1'd rather, weep."
"You show me love," smiled Romeo, "which sadly adds more grief,
To the grief already in my heart, for which I seek relief."

"Love is a smoke that's made from sighs, a madness that can fall,
It can be...oh, so very sweet, it can be...choking gall!
But enough of this, I leave you...now you have learned my pain."
"Before you go," Benvolio asked, "will you tell me your love's name?"

Romeo smiles and begins to describe his love.

"She has Diana's worldly wit, of her chastity, has proof,
Temptations do not move her, she has vowed to stand aloof,
Oh, such waste, for when she dies, her beauty dies as well,
She's cut it from prosperity, she leaves no one who can tell."

"She's fair and wise and finds no joy in making me despair,
She's foresworn love, she will not wed, so her vows I have to bear."
"Be ruled by me!" Benvolio said, "cast this woman from your mind,
Give liberty unto your eyes, look on others, don't be blind!"

"I cannot," answered Romeo, "I simply can't forget,
The treasures that my eyes beheld, 'fore blindness on me set.
I'll not forget dear cousin, you cannot teach me how."
"I will!" Benvolio told him, "my life… you have my vow!"

End of scene 1

Scene 2

Capulet is talking to Paris. A servant is nearby.

"Montague, as well as I, have been bound to keep the peace,
We both are old so surely now, this feud of ours can cease?"
"'Tis a pity," answered Paris, "you've lived at odds so long,
You've proved you both are honourable, let the enmity be
gone."

"But pray Lord, can you give me now, an answer to my plea,
That Juliet your daughter, be pledged to marry...me?"
"She's far too young," smiled Capulet, "your suit must be
denied,
Two more summers she must have, ere she's ripe to be a
bride."

"This earth has swallowed all my hopes, with her...they can
re-start,
So Paris, treat her gently, and thereby win her heart.
My consent to this is but a part, you must be her choice too,
Should she choose you...so will I, so go to her...and woo!"

"At my house tonight I host a feast, where many guests will
be,
You must come too, there will be girls I wish for you to see.
And once you have you may decide my daughter is too plain
And reconsider her your choice, and start to look again."

*Capulet gives the servant a list of the guests and tells him to
go to each house and give them the invitation.*

"Visit all those named upon this list, invite them all to come,
To a feast at my house where there'll be, much revelry and
fun."

Capulet exits, the servant looks at the list and mutters ...

"I am not learned, cannot read, but must find those listed here,
These lines to me mean nothing, however hard I peer!"

*He sees Benvolio and Romeo approaching and speaks to
them.*

"Good evening sirs, pray, can you read?" said Romeo "Ay, I
can."
"Then wilt thou read this list for me, that a route then I can
plan?"
Romeo read the list aloud, some noble, some of fame,
Then asked the servant, "Whose house is this? What is your
master's name?"

"Lord Capulet," he answered, "at his house, they will dine,
And if you're not a Montague, pray...join them for some
wine."
The servant exits, Benvolio speaks.
"Rosaline, the one you love, tonight is going there,
We must go too, your eyes to see, other beauties to compare!"

"Look first upon your loved one's face, and then on those I'll
show,
For I'm sure that when you've done so, you'll think your
swan...a crow!"
Smiling Romeo answered, "Nay, she's fairer than the sun,
There's not been one to match her, since first this world
began."

"You saw her first," said Benvolio, "with no others near that
shine,

Tonight you'll compare with other maids, the love that you call thine,"
"I'll go along," said Romeo, "not for others to be shown,
But to look upon the splendour of…the sight I call my own."

End of scene 2

Scene 3

Enter Lady Capulet who is speaking to the nurse.

"Send for my daughter Juliet, I have something I must say,"
The nurse calls for Juliet.
"Whilst waiting will you tell me, what age does she have today?"
"In two weeks' time," replied the nurse, "on the eve of Lammastide,
Fourteen years will then have passed, since first she breathed and cried."

The nurse continued talking, of Juliet's early years,
Her bruises, cuts, her falls, her fears, her laughter and her tears.
Her memories came flooding in, she could not make them cease,
'Til the Lady Capulet bade her, "Enough nurse, hold your peace."

Enter Juliet, the nurse greets her.

"'Tis my lovely babe, the one I nursed, the prettiest and the best,
I pray one day I'll see you wed, before I'm laid to rest."
Lady Capulet then demanded, "Of marriage have you thought?"
Juliet answered, "Mother…no, 'tis a dream I have not sought."

"Then start to think of marriage now," her mother firmly said,
"Some girls your age already have, a husband for their bed!
The valiant Paris seeks your love, and will woo you if he can,
He's a flower of Verona…could you favour such a man?"

"Tonight, he will attend our feast, where his face you will
behold,
Look closely on it, find delight, let his love for you unfold.
Look in the margins of his eyes, learn all he doth possess,
By taking him you will be whole…more and never less."

"I'll look upon him," Juliet said, "let my eye see what it will,
But I'll look no deeper than I must, my duty to fulfil."

Enter a serving man.

"Dinner is served," said the serving man, "pray enter now to
dine."
"Go sweet Juliet," cried the nurse, "may happiness be thine."

End of scene 3

Scene 4

Enter Romeo, Mercutio, Benvolio, other maskers and torchbearers. Romeo speaks.

"What excuse shall we give for intruding, or shall we give them none?"
"Let's not pretend," said Benvolio, "have our entrance openly done.
We'll not dress up like Cupid, and scare ladies with his bow,
As maskers, we'll do what we came for, then give them a dance, and go."

"I'm too sad to dance," sighed Romeo, "my soul feels full of lead,
I'm staked to the ground, my feet cannot move, my days of dancing...dead!"
"You're just in love!" Mercutio scoffed, "try using Cupid's wings,
Soar high above all others around, and see what soaring brings."

Said Romeo, "I cannot soar, higher than my sad woe,
Love's great burden makes me sink down, deeper and deeper I go.
Love isn't tender, it's rough, it's rude, it pricks me, like a thorn,
I'm dying of love, pierced with its shaft, of all other feelings...shorn."

They are still discussing this as they approach Capulet's house.

"If love treats you rough," said Mercutio, "you must be rough with love,
If it pricks you must return it, fight it, don't be a dove."

They are at the door.

We're here now, knock and we'll enter…soon as we're in, we must dance."
Romeo cried, "I'll carry the torch, you with light heels can prance."

"We'll not let you drown in your mire," Mercutio to Romeo said,
"But come, our time is burning away, through that door we must tread."
"No! do not enter," Romeo cried, "last night I had a dream,
It said it's unwise to go in there, the future, it has foreseen."

"I dreamt too," said Mercutio, "that dreamers often lie!"
"Yes…lie asleep," Romeo smiled, "but truth dreams cannot deny."
"I can tell you've had a visit…from Queen Mab," Mercutio said,
"The midwife of fairies, who, in the night, comes to spin tales in your head."

"She'll have a lover dreaming of love, a lawyer dreaming of fees,
A soldier will dream of the cutting of throats, swords and battles he sees.
Lightly, she'll touch on a woman's soft lips, who then will dream of a kiss,
She's a hag who gallops at night time, bringing dreamers their wish."

"Fantasy is the substance of dreams, born of a dull idle brain,
Holding no more than the air does…from dreams, nothing we gain."

"We'll all gain nothing," Benvolio warned, "time for us doesn't wait,
The evening is passing, supper is done, I fear we may be too late!"

"My mind is troubled," Romeo said, "a threat now hangs in the sky,
With this night's revels something will start, I know not what...or why,
I feel a vile untimely death, my breast is holding within,
But if this is fate...so be it...gentlemen, let us go in."
Disguised in their masks, they enter.

End of scene 4

Scene 5

Enter Capulet and his household, guests, Romeo, Benvolio, Mercutio and other maskers. Capulet greets everyone.

"Gentlemen, gentlemen, welcome, to this, my humble home,
The ladies here have carefree toes, you will not dance alone,
I've seen the day when masked I've danced, and whispered in an ear,
Alas that's all done, way in the past, some five and twenty years."

Capulet moves off to speak with his cousin whilst all the guests start to dance...except Romeo.

Romeo gazed upon the throng, then a lady caught his eye,
"Who's that?" he asked of a servant, "I don't know," was his reply.
"Oh!" cried Romeo, "She doth show torches how to burn bright,
A jewel hung rich upon an ear, she sparkles in the night."

"A snow white dove, whose beauty makes other maids seem like crows,
When this dance is done, I'll touch her hand, that her blessing through me flows.
'Til now I thought, that I had found love...that's...all gone from my sight,
I've never seen true beauty 'til...the beauty, seen tonight.'
Tybalt has been listening to Romeo and has recognised his voice. He is enraged.
"A Montague, within this house, how dare he?" Tybalt said,

"He flaunts us from behind a mask, my sword! This man is dead."
Capulet speaks to him.

"Why do you storm so kinsman, what makes your anger rise?"
"A Montague, here," raged Tybalt, "a foe in front of my eyes!"

Said Capulet, "'tis but Romeo, I'm told he is well bred,
Well-governed, truthful, virtuous, leave him, go calm your head.
This is my house, respect it, show prescience and good grace,
Be patient and endure him, take those frowns off your face."

"I'll not endure him," Tybalt snarled, "he's a villain, not a guest."
"YOU WILL," cried an angry Capulet, "my tolerance now you test.
Am I not the master of this house, or do you think it's you?
You defy me whilst among my guests, such a shameful thing to do."

"So again I say be quiet, or I'll make you keep the peace,
Do not defy me further sir, put your anger on a leash."
Tybalt glares at him.
"You force calmness on me Uncle, so yes…I will withdraw,
But his intrusion deeply riles me, it is bitter in my craw!"
He storms out.

Romeo approaches Juliet, he takes her hand and speaks to her.

"I offer my unworthy hand, if too rough…I promise, this,
My lips are here to smooth away, that roughness, with a kiss."
"Good pilgrim," Juliet answered, "you wrong your hand too much,
You hand in mine is happiness, I feel pleasure in its touch."

"Do not saints have lips," he asked her, "and palmers coming home?"
"Ay," she answered "lips they have, that in prayer they may atone."
"Then dear saint," smiled Romeo, "a prayer my lips will make,
Do not move, be patient, as my prayer's effect, I take." *He kisses her.*

"Thus, your lips have purged my sins, with a gentle touch from mine,"
"So now," she smiled, "my lips must have, the sins that once were thine."
"They cannot trespass there," he cried, "give me back my sins again!"
He kisses her once more.
She laughed and said, "You kiss by the book, I felt not any pain!"

The nurse approaches and speaks to Juliet.

"Your mother craves a word with you, pray go to her right now."
Juliet moves away.
"Who is her mother?" Romeo asked, "that I may make my bow?"
"My good mistress," answered the nurse, "the lady of this house,
Much wealth awaits the man who takes, her daughter as his spouse."

She exits and Romeo speaks to Benvolio.

"I fear she is a Capulet, my new love is…a foe!"
Benvolio urged, "The game is done, it's time for us to go."
Capulet sees them leaving.

"Are you leaving now? called Capulet, "I thank you, and goodnight,
It waxes late, to my bed to rest, come servant bring me light."

They all leave except Juliet and the nurse. Juliet points to Romeo and speaks.

"Before he leaves, go ask his name, for he has turned my head,
The nurse runs off.
If he's married then my grave will be my empty wedding bed."
The nurse returned and said, "My dear, his name is Romeo,
The only son of Montague, your family's greatest foe!"

"My only love," sobbed Juliet, "sprung from my only hate,
the love so new, within my breast, is already now too late.
What was born today is oh so cruel, that I should love a foe."
"Come," said the nurse, "that is enough, it's sad…but we must go."

End of scene 5
End of ACT 1

Act 2
Scene 1

Enter Romeo walking away from the Capulet's house. He speaks.

"I cannot walk on when my heart is here,
Turn back, return, to the one I hold dear."
He climbs a wall back into Capulet's garden.

Enter Benvolio and Mercutio, looking for Romeo. Mercutio speaks.

"He's not a fool and is probably now home asleep in his bed."
"But he climbed that wall to their garden, I saw him," Benvolio said.
"Call him Mercutio, call him again, then we'll say our goodbyes."
"I'll conjure him up!" Mercutio laughed. "Let's see if his spirit replies."

"Spirit of Romeo speak or appear." There came not a single reply.
"He's deep in the trees," Benvolio said, "in league with night's moody sky.
His love is blind and best befits, the night-time and it's dark."
"If his love is so blind," Mercutio said, "it will never hit its mark!"

"This field is too cold for sleeping, so home to my own warm bed,

Goodnight, good luck, dear Romeo, let not your heart rule your head."

"Yes," said Benvolio, "let us withdraw, it's clear he's gone to ground,

It's pointless to search any more here, he has no wish to be found."

They exit.
Romeo is in the Capulet's garden in the trees, looking up at a balcony. Juliet appears and Romeo speaks to himself.

"What light through yonder window breaks? 'tis Juliet, the sun,

Arise fair sun, kill the pale moon, she's sick, her time is done.
You are her maid yet far fairer, so be her maid…no more,
Cast off her green vestal clothing, that you, may open love's door."

"There is my true love, my lady, Oh! If she knew she were,
Should I speak now and tell her? No…too bold…do not stir.
For I think 'tis not me she talks to, but stars ablaze in the skies,
They cannot match the glow of her cheek or the light I see in her eyes."

Juliet now speaks aloud.

"O Romeo, my Romeo, where are you Romeo?
Deny your father, shun his name, those earthly ties…let go,
But if you find that you cannot, my dear one do not fret,
Just swear by our love and I will be…no longer…Capulet!"

"Only your name is my enemy, naught else of what is you,
You are yourself, could never change, were you not a Montague.
What's in a name? for would not a rose, if called by some other word,
Smell just as sweet just as fragrant, to think not…is so absurd."

"If you were not called Romeo, you would still...perfection be,
So take no title, doff your name, it is not part of thee.
You need no name, instead take me, as your true and only love, *Romeo burst out speaking!*
"I do! I do!" he cried aloud, "What joy I hear from above."

Juliet is startled, unaware that she has been overheard.

"What man would use night as a screen, to stumble on my thought?"
"I know not what to say," he cried, "my name makes me distraught.
I find it so distasteful, for it has become your foe."
"I know that voice," she murmured, "are you not...Romeo?"

"How came you here? these walls are high; in this place you should not tread.
For if my kinsmen find you here, you surely would be dead!"
"I flew the walls," he answered, "with the lightness of love's wings,
Your kinsmen cannot stop love's work, or the future that it brings."

"If they see you they will kill you, that must not be," she cried.
He smiled and said, "their eyes won't see...in the cloak of night, I'll hide.
But if you do not love me, then let them find me here,
I'd rather die by their hand now, than never have you near."
"Oh, Romeo," she answered, "night's mask is on my face,
Were it not you'd see the blushes, revealing my disgrace,
For what you heard me say tonight, I should have later said,
After courtship and formalities, all have had their head."

"But what I said, is said now, form does not apply,
So I ask again, do you love me? to which, you'll answer aye.

31

For things are said when love is young, that could later prove untrue,
Oh gentle love, pray say those words, I hope you'll never rue."

"Perhaps you think I'm easily won, to which I tell you no!
I should have been far more reserved…that you heard…I did not know
So pardon me for what was said, I was speaking to the night,
And do not think the thoughts expressed were frivolous and light."

"By yonder moon I vow," he said, "that which I say to you."
She interrupted crying, "No…! The moon can be untrue.
Throughout the month she circles round. Each day a different face,
I fear your love will likewise prove, then die without a trace."

"In my love for you I find much joy, but not in our pledge tonight,
It is too rash, too sudden come, and quickly could take flight,
So let our bud of love mature, each warming summer hour,
That when we meet again 'twill be…a wondrous blooming flower."

She bids him goodnight…he calls to her.

"Will you leave me here unsatisfied? To do so is unkind."
"What could I give," she answered, "that satisfaction you would find?"
"The exchange of faithful vows," he said, "now our love has been unmasked."
"I already gave you mine," she smiled," before you even asked!"

The nurse calls from within. Juliet speaks quietly.

"Adieu dear love, I must go in but ask that you await,

I will return to speak with you, to talk more about our fate."
She exits and Romeo speaks alone
"Oh blessed night," he whispered, "but fear because it's night
It's all a dream, it is not true, and will vanish with the light!"

Juliet returns, and speaks.

"If all you've said is honour bound...to an altar we will tread,
Send word tomorrow morning, of where, and when, we'll wed.
Then my life and all my fortune, before you I will lay,
And I, my lord, will follow you, forever and a day."

"So once again I say goodnight...but parting is sweet sorrow,
Again, then again, I'll say it 'til...night, becomes tomorrow."
She exits and Romeo calls after her
"Sleep to your eyes peace to your breast...but hence I must away,
To my friar's house my tale to tell, that he help me now...I pray."

He exits.
End of scene 1

Scene 2

Enter friar Lawrence carrying a basket and speaking his thoughts.

"The morning smiles and frowns on night, the sun now turns its eye
To bum away the darkness, turn dew from dank to dry.
This basket I must fill today, with the bounty of earth's womb,
That children from earth's plants and herbs, find succour in their bloom."

Enter Romeo who greets the friar. The friar speaks to him.

"Your earliness tells me you're awake, due to sickness of the head,
Or, what is much more likely is, you have not been to bed!
If so were you with Rosaline?" "I was not," said Romeo,
"I have forgotten that maid's name…it gave me so much woe!"

"Where have you been?" the friar asked, "that you were out all night?"
"At a feast with my foe," said Romeo, which has filled me with delight.
For I met and wooed the daughter, of the rich lord Capulet,
I gave my vow and she gave hers, our intentions are now set."

"We wish to enter marriage, and father, here I pray,
You'll hear my plea and then consent, to marry us this day."

"Oh holy saints!" the father cried, "what change do we have here,
Is Rosaline forsaken now, the one you held so dear?"

"So many tears just fell to waste, washing down your cheek,
For Rosaline...who you pursued, whose love you tried to seek."
Said Romeo, "Don't chide me so, it seems you have forgot,
Whilst my new love truly loves me...Rosaline did not."

The friar considers for a while and then speaks.

"Very well then," friar Lawrence said, "I will perform this rite,
This alliance may so happy prove, your households will unite."
"So let us hence," cried Romeo, "I'm in haste to have it done."
"Go wise, and slow," the father said, "they stumble who would run."

End of scene 2

Scene 3

Enter Benvolio and Mercutio. Mercutio speaks.

"Where the devil is our Romeo, did he not come home last night?"
"I was told by his man," Benvolio said, "of Romeo there's no sight.
That Rosaline torments him so, he's forever low and sad,
She's naught but a cold, hard-hearted wench, who will surely drive him mad."

"And now he has been challenged, by letter to a duel,
The challenge comes from Tybalt, who at fencing, is no fool.
But Romeo will answer it by matching Tybalt's dare."
"That worries me," cried Mercutio, "his thoughts are so elsewhere."

"Rosaline crowds his heart and mind, he's in no state to fight,
He must not answer Tybalt's dare, 'til his mind is clear and bright.
For Tybalt learned his duelling, at the finest duelling school,
Romeo's good and fearless, let's hope he's not a fool!"

Enter Romeo who is greeted, then questioned by his friends.

They asked him "Where were you all night, what made you slip away?"
They teased and made much fun of him, in the way that friends oft' play.
But Romeo returned their jests, and in good measure too,

To them he seemed quite sharp again, like the Romeo they knew.

Enter the nurse and her man, Peter. Mercutio sees them, and makes fun of their appearance.

"What comes here, can they be sails, or just a shirt and smock?
I hope she'll use her fan to hide a face that's quite a shock!"
"Good morrow, sirs," she greeted them, "or has the morning fled?"
"The clock's hand is on the prick of noon...morn's gone," Mercutio said.

"A saucy answer," said the nurse, "but who can tell me where,
I may find young Romeo, I have something I must share."
"I, am he," said Romeo, "what is it you would say?"
"I will tell you, sir," she answered, "when your friends have moved away."

"She's wooing you!" Benvolio laughed, "she'll ask you home to dine,
So we'll leave you now, but do beware...she's way beyond her prime.
Farewell dear ancient lady, farewell! farewell, farewell!
We'll meet you later Romeo, at the sound of the dinner bell."
They exit laughing.

"Who was that man?" she hotly asked, "so full of saucy talk,"
"A gentleman," said Romeo, "who speaks more than he ought."
"A scurvy knave!" the nurse replied, "who'd best not speak 'gainst me,
For if he does, I'll take him down, I've downed better men than he!"

"I've said enough so let me turn, to why I'm here today,
But before I do, there's something else, I feel that I should say,

My lady's young and gentle sir, pray, do not double deal,
For to lead her in fool's paradise, would cause pain that could
not heal."

"I must protest," cried Romeo, "my intentions are most pure,
I'll never, ever, lead her, to pain that has no cure."
"She will be joyous," smiled the nurse, "I'll tell her you'll be
true,
You are indeed a gentleman, there is nothing she will rue."

"And tell her this," smiled Romeo, "come here this afternoon.
For then, we will be married, in the holy father's room."
"We shall be there," the nurse replied, "in wedding clothes
adorned,
But one last word before I go, for I think you should be
warned."

"You've a rival here, a nobleman, and Paris is his name,
He also seeks my lady's hand, and indeed, has laid a claim."
"I thank you nurse," said Romeo, "I'm warned by what you
said,
So hasten now, go fetch my bride, that quickly we may wed."

They exit.
End of scene 3

Scene 4

Enter Juliet. She is anxiously awaiting the return of the nurse who has been visiting Romeo.

"She said she'd be but half an hour, it's been now almost three,
Perhaps she missed him, perhaps she's lame, what can the problem be?
Love's heralds should be as arrows, flying quickly to and fro,
My nurse alas, lacks youthful blood, she's unwieldy, heavy, slow."

The nurse enters.

"Oh! Sweet nurse what news do you bring, pray tell me, good or bad?
If bad then tell me…merrily, if good, why look so sad?"
"I'm weary now," explained the nurse, "please let me pause and rest,
My bones all ache, I'm out of breath, I sorely have been pressed."

"You've breath to tell me you've no breath, how strange," cried Juliet,
"To tell me that, took longer than, the news I hope to get!
So…tell me now, no more delay…is it good, or is it not?
Just tell me plainly, yes or no…what answer have I got?"

The nurse sighs and reluctantly answers.
"Your choice of man is most unwise, many troubles I foresee,
But…to other men, your Romeo, compares most favourably.

His face is handsome, body strong, a fair picture of a man,
He lacks in manners, but I'm sure, is as gentle, as a lamb."

"I know all that," cried Juliet, "what of our plans to wed?"
"I'd quite forgotten," moaned the nurse, 'tis the aching in my head!
And my poor poor back, so painful, this jaunting has me bruised,
In future you can go yourself, I'll no longer be misused!"

She smiles, then continues.

"But although I ache, I'll give you news, that will surely change your life,
Go to the friar's house today, where, you'll become a wife!
Whilst you do I'll find a ladder, more toil for your delight, So your love can climb it later, and visit you this night."

End of scene 4

Scene 5

Enter friar Lawrence and Romeo. The friar speaks.

"Let heaven smile upon this act, and sadness never follow."
"Amen to that," said Romeo, "but if it comes tomorrow
It could never dim the joy I'll feel, when we kneel within your shrine,
And you join our hands in marriage, and I know, that she is mine."

The friar counselled, "Pace your love, too swift, and it may die,
Just love in moderation, never low, and never high.
Enter Juliet.
Ah! here comes your lovely lady, how light of foot her tread,
She'd never scratch a flint stone or break a cobweb's thread."

"Oh Juliet!" cried Romeo, "if your joy is heaped like mine,
Make sweet the air and tell me, you feel this day…divine."
"Sweet Romeo," she answered, "mere words could not express,
The depth and value of my love…it has grown to such excess!"

The friar interrupts.

"Oh! Come, come now," said the father, "this is no time to woo,
Pray pardon me, we all must go, there's much that we must do.
I cannot leave you here alone, unless my work is done,

And through me the church combines you…forevermore, as one!"

The exit together.

End of scene 5
End of ACT 2

Act 3
Scene 1

Mercutio and Benvolio are walking in town. Benvolio speaks.

"The day is hot, our foes are near, pray let us both go home,
If we meet them there will be a brawl, foul words and punches
thrown."
"Go home my friend?" Mercutio laughed, "that doesn't sound
like you,
You look for quarrels, seek them out, it's what you always
do!"

"I've seen you argue with a man, 'bout the beard upon his
face,
And another who had tied his shoes with ribbon, not a lace,
And a man who coughed, and woke your dog, who lay
sleeping at your feet,
Your head is full of quarrels man, like an egg is full of meat."

Enter Tybalt and other Capulets. Benvolio sees them.

"By my oath here come the Capulets, it seems they wish to
speak,
This place is public, eyes that watch, somewhere private we
should seek."
"Let eyes watch," Mercutio said, "I'll not budge from off this
spot,
If Tybalt wants to speak with us, he must do it here…or not!"
As Tybalt is talking to Mercutio, Romeo enters.

"Ah, here comes my man," said Tybalt, "the one I wish to see,
You are a villain Romeo, that's what I think of thee!"
"Tybalt," Romeo answered, "with rage I should reply,
There's a reason that I cannot, so I bid you sir goodbye!"

"That does not excuse," said Tybalt, "the pain you've brought
to me,
So turn and draw, I will avenge, your blatant villainy."
"I do protest," cried Romeo, "I've never caused you harm,
I offer love, I will not draw, I beg you sir, be calm."

Mercutio looks at Romeo astonished.

"What dishonour!" cried Mercutio, "to submit like this is vile,
If you won't fight he wins and walks, the thought just raises
bile.
Tybalt, hold! wil't stand 'gainst me? be quick or I will strike."
"Aye, I'll stand sir," Tybalt growled, "nothing better would I
like."
They fight. Romeo tries to stop them.

"Put up your sword Mercutio, good Tybalt, raise yours too,
This shameful outrage must stop now, or more trouble will
ensue.
Against fighting in Verona's streets, the Prince has firmly
found,
Benvolio...will you help me, beat their swords unto the
ground."

*Together they use their swords to try and beat the others
down.*
*From behind Romeo, Tybalt stabs Mercutio and then flees the
scene. Mercutio cries out.*
"A plague on both your houses, they have caused me mortal
harm,
Why did you come between us? I was stabbed beneath your
arm."

"I thought it best," sobbed Romeo, "so it wouldn't end this way."
"I'm worm's meat now," Mercutio sighed," I'll not see another, day."
He is carried away to die.

Romeo is alone and muses.

"A friend lies with a mortal wound, and I must take the blame,
He drew his sword on my behalf, I am mortified with shame,
Sweet Juliet, my love for you, has made my senses reel,
It has weakened my poor manliness, and softened valour's steel."

Benvolio enters to tell Romeo of Mercutio's death.

"Oh Romeo our friend is gone, Mercutio is dead,
His time on earth so soon is spent, to the clouds his spirit fled."
"This day's black fate," said Romeo, "on more days now depends,
Now has begun the dreadful woe, that other days must end."
Romeo sees an angry Tybalt returning and speaks to Benvolio about Tybalt.

"Alive…in triumph, Mercutio dead, and now to heaven gone,
Hot fury will now be my guide, of mercy I'll show none.
Tybalt stay, take back your charge, that I…a villain be,
Mercutio's soul awaits above, for either you, or me!"

They fight and Tybalt is slain. Benvolio cries to Romeo.

"Romeo, quick, be gone from here, the citizens draw near,
With Tybalt's body lying there, they'll want your head I fear.
The Prince will carry out his threat, you will be doomed to death,
Why do you linger? go at once, don't even stop for breath."

Romeo flees. The Prince enters with senior Montagues and Capulets and other citizens. The Prince demands.

"Benvolio, who was it that began this bloody fray?"
"'twas Tybalt Prince," Benvolio said, "he was the first to slay.
Tybalt challenged Romeo, but he refused to draw,
Mercutio, angered, took his place, and at Tybalt fiercely tore."

"Romeo begged them both to stop, and bravely stood between,
Which alas gave the chance to Tybalt, to strike his foe unseen.
Mercutio died and Tybalt fled, but later, did return,
Where Romeo, now man again, for revenge did hotly burn."

"They went to it then like lightning, swords ringing like a bell,
Before I could try to part them, stout Tybalt cried…and fell.
And as he did young Romeo, did turn about and fly,
My Prince, I swear, this all is truth, or let Benvolio die!"
Lady Capulet speaks to the Prince.

"He's kinsman of a Montague, and so is speaking false,
The law is clear on what should be…the law should take its course,
So hear my plea for justice, which I beg you Prince to give,
Romeo slew our Tybalt, Romeo should not live."

"Blood was spilled," the Prince replied, then blood was spilled again,
Need there be more, to end all this? NO! my answer's plain.
For his offence, young Romeo, from this city is outcast,
Should he not comply and then is found…that hour will be his last!"

"Mercutio was of my blood, so I have suffered too.
For this you all will pay strong fines, you'll repent and pay your due.
I will be deaf to pleading, my mind will not be changed,

Now, bear this body out from here, have interment now arranged."
They all exit.

End of scene 1

Scene 2

Juliet is alone, not knowing what has happened.

"Oh Romeo, the night draws near, come soon unto my arms,
You have bought the mansion of my love, but not yet known its charms.
I am sold but yet, am not possessed, this day is hard to bear,
I'm like a child that has new clothes, but which, I cannot wear."

The nurse enters, very upset.

"Why do you wring your hands so nurse, why do you look severe?
What news is it you bring me, is it news I should not hear?"
"He's dead my lady," wailed the nurse, "he's dead, he's gone, he's killed,
Oh damn this day, we are undone, he's dead…his blood is spilled."

"You torture me," cried Juliet, "what is it you would say?
Did Romeo take his own sweet life? Torment me not this way.
If he is slain then just say…ay, if not, then tell me…no,
What you say now will determine, my happiness…or woe."

"Mine own eyes saw his bleeding chest, 'twas awful," said the nurse,
"Such a gory corpse, bedaubed In blood, my life! I've not seen worse.

I swooned at the very sight of it, and longed to find my bed,
Oh courteous Tybalt, gentle man, who thought I'd see you
dead?"

Juliet is bewildered and demands an explanation.

"What contrary storm is this now, that you appear to blow,
Is my cousin and my lord dead, will you add unto, my woe?"
"'tis Tybalt dead," the nurse replied, "and Romeo sent away,
It was Romeo who slew Tybalt, with exile he must pay."

Juliet is dismayed and is, at first, angry with Romeo.

"Oh serpent head," she murmured, "hid with a flowering face,
A dragon living in a cave, that's such a wondrous place,
A book with contents vile and foul, and yet…so finely bound,
How could deceit so awful be, in such a palace found?"

"These griefs and sorrows," moaned the nurse, "combine to
make me old,
"Romeo now is drenched in shame, what pain he's made
unfold."
"Nurse, hold your tongue," snapped Juliet, "he was not born
to shame,
His brow is a throne where shame would be, ashamed to leave
its stain."

"What a beast I was to chide him, to let such thoughts begin."
Surprised, the nurse asked "you'd speak well…of the man
who killed your kin?"
"Should I speak ill," said Juliet, "of the man who I did wed,
Of he that is my husband, who…my cousin wanted dead?"

"No! So foolish tears back to your spring, my husband is
alive,
But forever banished from this land, what worse can fate
contrive?

I will die a widowed maiden, so…to my wedding bed,
There death and not my husband, will take my maidenhead."

"Go to your chamber," said the nurse, "and I'll find Romeo,
And bring him to your room tonight, that you some comfort know,
I'll go to where he's hiding now, at the friar's holy cell."
"Bid him quickly come," sobbed Juliet, "for one last, sad farewell."

They exit.

End of scene 2

Scene 3

Enter the friar and Romeo.

"Oh Romeo, you fearful man, it seems where e'r you go,
Calamity will follow you…it's all you'll ever know.
For the crime that you've committed, you have been exiled hence,
Between this town and you my son, the Prince has placed a fence."

"I'm exiled…hence?" cried Romeo, "why death would be more kind,
To be exiled holds more terror, than death could ever find.
Outside our walls there is no world, except the world of hell,
So cut off my head and I will smile, for I will have died then…well."

"Such ingratitude," the friar said, "the law demands you die,
But the Prince, in kindness, mercy showed, and the law he'll not apply."
"Hear me father," Romeo begged, "what banishment really means,
Naught but torture all my life, for I'll never live my dreams."

"Heaven is where Juliet lives, with the creatures we all love,
The dogs, the cats, each little mouse, the birds that fly above.
Upon her they may look each day, but Romeo…may not,
I am banished down to hell, and slowly there will rot!"

"Father, have you any poison mixed, or a keenly sharpened blade?

The sudden means to end my life, which for exile, I would trade."
Alarmed, the father cried, "No, No, 'tis a sin to think this way,
In exile comfort can be found, hear what I have to say."

"You cannot speak," sighed Romeo, "of that you do not feel,
You need be young and so in love, your head, with love, doth reel.
Then one hour wed, you kill a man, and be banished who knows where?
Only then can you speak, or maybe, rage, fall down and tear your hair!"

He falls, weeping.

There is an urgent knocking on the door. The friar speaks to Romeo.

"Romeo, quickly, hide yourself, there is knocking at the door,
To my study, run or be taken, go hide or face the law.
"Who's that who knocks, and why so loud, why cause you such a din?
"I'm from Juliet," the nurse called out, "with a message, let me in."
she enters.

"Oh holy father, tell me please, where is my lady's lord?"
"There, on the floor," he answered, "drunk with the tears he's poured."
"My mistress too," the nurse replied, "she does naught but wail and weep,
For your lady's sake sir, rise and stand, let not your manhood sleep."
"Does Juliet think," asked Romeo, "that I a murderer be?
That I have stained our love with blood, from her own kin's family tree?"
"She does nothing sir," replied the nurse, "'cept lie weeping, on her bed,

She'll call Tybalt's name, then Romeo's, then beats upon her head."

"My cur-sed name!" cried Romeo, "is killing my sweet wife,
If my name was in my body, I'd remove it with a knife."
"You cry like a woman," the friar said, "yet your form says you are man,
I thought you were of sterner stuff, are you only bluff and sham?"

"Rouse yourself! your Juliet lives, be happy that is so,
Be happy too the law forgave, just exile you will know.
A pack of blessings lie in wait, and happiness will shine,
You could ponder on the good to come, but all you do is…whine!"

"Don't wallow in such misery, take heed of what I've said,
Go! get thee to your lady's room, and the comfort of her bed.
But, be careful not to stay too long, make sure a watch is set,
Next morning, pass to Mantua, that your exile terms are met."

"Whilst you live there we will rally friends, and seek pardon for your crime,
That the Prince allow you come home soon, in the shortest span of time.
So nurse, away to your lady go, prepare her for her lord."
"I'll leave at once," the nurse replied, "your counsel I applaud."
she exits.
"Oh how my spirits are restored, what joy," smiled Romeo,
"But tonight take care," the friar warned, "by dawning you must go
So to your wife, then Mantua, when things happen, I'll send news,
Give me your hand then go with God, and…always seek his views."
End of scene 3

Scene 4

Enter Capulet, his wife and Paris who asks about his proposal. Capulet speaks.

"I've not spoken to our daughter yet, events have stolen time,
Your proposal stays unknown to her, of your love, she's had no sign,
She's in her room, the hour is late, she'll not come down till light."
"I understand," the count replied, "so I'll bid you both goodnight."

"By early morn," said Capulet, "her mind-set we will see,
But you may rest assured dear count, she will be ruled by me!"
Wife, go now to her chamber, tell her all that this man brings,
And bid her mark next Thursday morn, for exchange of wedding rings."

"We will keep it small, without much fuss, with just a friend or two,
We are still in mourning for our kin, to be brash would never do.
What say you to next Thursday count? perhaps that is too soon?"
"My lord," smiled Paris, "all I wish, is that Thursday quickly bloom."

"That's settled then," said Capulet, "on Thursday you will wed,

Go now wife to our daughter's room, and prepare for what's
ahead.
Farewell dear count, I'll say goodnight, it's almost break of
day,
I'm tired now, so bring me light, to my bed I must away."

End of scene 4

Scene 5

Romeo and Juliet are in her bedroom. A bird sings and Juliet speaks.

"Are you going now? it is not day, we've not yet heard the lark,
'twas the nightingale you heard just then, still singing in the dark,"
"It was the lark," smiled Romeo, "the herald of the morn,
I must go to live, stay...I die...clouds part, to show the dawn."

"That's not dawn's light," she pleaded, "oh stay my lord please stay."
"I would rather stay than go," he said, "so shall stay, come what may.
Let me be taken, put to death, pay the price asked by the law,
If that's your wish, then I'm content, so let us talk some more."
Juliet is alarmed.

"No, No, I'm wrong," in fright she cried, *"that* is the dawn I see,
You cannot stay, be gone from here, you will be seen...so flee!"
"More light adds darkness to our woes, I'll go," said Romeo,
"But one last kiss before I do, that your lips, once more, I'll know," *They kiss*

The nurse enters and warns Juliet her mother is on the way. Juliet calls to Romeo as he climbs down.

"Oh Romeo my lord and love, do you think we'll meet again?"
"I doubt it not," he answered, "and there will be less pain,
For the woes we have, in time will pass, and fade in memory."
"Oh god," she cried, "let that be so, for it's not now what I see."

"My eyes look down upon you, as if dead, within a tomb,
You look so pale it frightens me, and I fear I see our doom."
"We both look pale," he answered, "our blood is drained by sorrow,
Have faith my love, now I must go...believe in our tomorrow."

Enter lady Capulet who speaks to Juliet.

"I see you are awake and up, perhaps you are not well?"
"Indeed I'm not," said Juliet, "but why, I cannot tell."
"You weep too much for your cousin," said lady Capulet,
"Have done with that, you've shown your love, no longer grieve and fret."

"I think you may be weeping, not for your cousin's death,
But that the villain who did slay him, is still living drawing breath."
"What villain's that?" asked Juliet, "does that villain have a name?"
"Why, Romeo," her mother cried "now gone from here in shame."

"We will have vengeance have no fear, so daughter do not weep,
I have a man in Mantua, with means to make men 'sleep'!
One dose of his cruel mixture, and our villain will be gone,
I hope you'll then be satisfied, with this matter sealed and done."

Juliet answers in a manner to give, but disguise her feelings for Romeo.

"Satisfied? no hardly so, but would be should I see
Romeo's 'sleeping' body, after poisoning by me!
Get me that poison mother, such a mixture I'd prepare,
That quickly he'd be 'sleeping', whilst I said for him a prayer,"

Oh, how I hate to hear his name, and know I can't begin,
To wreak upon his body, the love I bore my kin,"
"Go, find the means," her mother said, "the poison I'll obtain,
But first I bring you joyous news, to sweep away your pain."

"Your father has prepared for you, a wondrous happy day,
On Thursday morn at St. Peter's church, he'll there, give you away,
To the gallant, noble Paris, who will take you as his bride,
Who from that day forth will be your lord, your husband and your guide."

"He will not!" she answered angrily, "can this news you bring be true?
What haste is this, that I must wed, before he's called to woo?
I'd rather marry Romeo, he you know I hate,
Than the nobleman count Paris, who will never be my mate!"

Enter Capulet and the nurse. Capulet speaks.
"How now my wife, have you given her, the news of our decree?"
"Indeed I have," she answered, "she declines with thanks to thee."
"What's this you say?" cried Capulet, "you tell me she's declined?
Refused the one I brought to her? how unworthy, how unkind."

"Pray hear me father," Juliet wept, "for I could never be,
Proud to wed as you demand, 'twould be hurtful, false to me."
"Proud or not," roared Capulet, "on Thursday you will wed,
I will drag you there if needs be, to the altar you will tread!"

"Dear God in heaven," cried the nurse, "you should not scold
her so."
"Hold your tongue," he harshly snapped, "or to your gossips
go."
"May I not speak?" the nurse replied, "no!" he thundered
back,
"Be quiet now you mumbling fool, sense you surely lack."

Juliet falls on her knees before him.

"Good father mine," cried Juliet, "I beg you, on my knees,
Hear my heartfelt pleading, be patient with me please."
He stopped her shouting, "No, you wretch, instead hear what
I say,
On Thursday morn, be at the church, or this is how you'll
pay."

"You'll not look upon my face again, you'll not share my
house with me,
You'll have to graze where' ere you can...I do not jest with
thee.
Think carefully on what I've said, my words I'll not take back,
Do what I ask on Thursday morn, and never will you lack."
"But should you not, you'll be disowned, to starve upon the
street,
I never will acknowledge you, whatever ills you meet,
What I now have shall not be yours, your bridges will be
burned,
So again I say, think carefully, my mind will not be turned."
he exits

Juliet appeals to her mother.

"Oh sweet mother, do not spurn me, stop this wedding, hear my cries,
If you can't then make my wedding bed, in the grave where Tybalt lies."
"Talk not to me," her mother said, "for I'll not say a word,
Do as you wish, I'm done with you, your pleading goes unheard."
She exits Juliet turns to the nurse.

"How shall this be prevented nurse, can you tell me what to do?"
"I can my child," the nurse replied, "here's good advice for you.
Your Romeo, is banned from here and is never to return,
He cannot come to claim his wife, if he does, in hell, he'll burn."

"Count Paris is a worthy man, it's he you should now wed,
Compared to him your Romeo, is a dishrag toe to head!
This second match excels the first, which is dead, no further use,
Use these thoughts from my heart and head, to save yours from the noose!"

"You comfort me," said Juliet, "tell my mother I'll now go,
To the friar, to get pardon for, displeasing father so."
"This is so wise," replied the nurse, "I will go at once to tell.
You have gone to make confession, be absolved of sin as well."

The nurse exits and Juliet glares after her whilst cursing her.
"Damnation on you, wicked fiend, my husband you praised high,
And now you do the opposite…we're finished you and I.
The friar will tell me what to do, he'll guide me from this strife,

But if he fails my remedy is…to end my own short life."

End of scene 5

End of ACT 3

Act 4

Scene 1

Enter friar Lawrence and count Paris. The friar speaks.

"The wedding you say is Thursday, but the bride has not agreed,
I do not like this undue haste, why should there be such speed?"
"She weeps too much," the count replied, "o'er the death of her slain kin,
Her father thinks if she's soon wed, her joy will then begin."

Juliet enters, Paris greets her.

"Greetings my sweet and gentle maid, who soon I will call 'wife',
Yes, Thursday morn, we will be wed, and begin our married life.
Have you come to make confession, of sins on earth be free?
One confession I know you'll make, is that you, my dear, love me."

"To do that would be meaningless, so…I won't," said Juliet,
"But wish to speak with the father, his counsel I must get."
"I'll not disturb you," Paris said, "but this, I wish to say,
On Thursday morn I'll rouse you, for our joyous wedding day."

Paris exits and Juliet, crying, speaks to the friar.

"Weep with me father, feel my grief, I'm past hope, past help, past care."
"I do my child," he answered, "of your plight, I am aware."
"Then tell me what to do?" she cried, "this wedding to deny,
If you in your wisdom can't tell me…then father, I must die!"
She draws out a knife.

"God joined my heart with Romeo's, our hands were joined by you,
Thus heart and hands were tightly sealed, to ne'er be split in two.
If against my will I have to give, another man my vow,
I'd free my hands and kill our hearts…with this knife, that I hold, now."

"No! wait my child," the father urged, "I do espy some hope,
If you have the nerve to die now, with my plan you'll surely cope.
It's a plan that looks like death itself, it will keep you free from shame,
If you are willing to risk it, then listen, I'll explain."

Juliet is overjoyed.

"Oh anything father, anything. That Paris and I don't wed,
I'd jump from a tower, battle through snakes, in a charnel house I'd bed!
Whatever needs be done I'll do, without any doubt or fear,
That I may be an unstained wife, to the one that I hold dear."

"Very well then," said the father, "go home and be contrite,
Agree to marry Paris but…late on Wednesday night,
Be on your own in your chamber, and when you are in bed,
Drink all this vial of liquid, and on your pillow lay your head."

"Soon, you will feel very drowsy, your heart will lose its beat,
Colour from lips and cheeks will fade, you'll have neither breath nor heat,

You'll be stiff and cold, quite deathlike, unconsciousness, very deep,
Two days will pass then you will stir, and waken as from sleep."

"Then on Thursday morn when Paris calls, to rouse you from your bed,
He'll find that you're not sleeping, he'll find that you are 'dead'.
As is custom in our country, you'll be robed and tributes paid,
Then in the ancient family vault, that day, you will be laid."

"While you are sleeping, I will send for Romeo to come,
Together we'll watch and guard you, till all your sleeping's done.
That very night he'll take you away, to together live as one,
If you have the nerve to do this, then shame you will have none."

She takes the vial and they exit.

End of scene 1

Scene 2

Enter Capulet, his wife and serving men. He is issuing instructions for the wedding.

Capulet sent his serving men this that and every way,
To ensure that all was perfect for a perfect wedding day.
Turning to the nurse he asked, "Has my daughter yet returned?
Let's hope the friar's counsel worked, and her thinking has been turned."

Juliet enters and pretends obedience. Capulet speaks to her.

"Where have you been, you headstrong girl? Pray tell me where you went."
"To where I learned," she answered, "that my sins I must repent
She falls to her knees.
I ask you for your pardon sir, for disobeying you,
Henceforth, I will be ruled by you, what 'ere you want I'll do."

"I'm overjoyed," laughed Capulet, "call the count that I may say,
This knot will be tied tomorrow, I'll advance it by a day.
Nurse take my daughter to her room, and there select her dress,
Go with them wife help deck her out...for tomorrow's happiness."

His wife complained, "so much to do, it's late and almost light."

"All will be well," he answered, "I'll work throughout the night.

But first to the count to warn him, to prepare for early morn,

How wondrous light my head is, now my daughter is re-born."

He exits.

End of scene 2

Scene 3

Juliet, her mother and the nurse are in Juliet's chamber. She speaks.

"We have chosen all that's wanted, for tomorrow's solemn day,
So mother, nurse, please leave me now, there is no need to stay.
I must have time alone to pray, that the heavens on me smile,
And I'm sure that you have much to do, so go now, rest a while."

They leave saying 'goodnight'. Juliet speaks her thoughts.

"Farewell mother, farewell nurse, will we ever meet, again?
Cold fear flows quickly through me now, freezing every vein.
I could call them back for comfort but…what good would doing that do?
She takes out the vial.
This dismal scene I must do alone, come vial, be strong, and true."

"But…what if this mixture does not work, will tomorrow I be wed?
Or…has the father mixed things so, tomorrow I'll be dead!?
What if I wake too early, and Romeo isn't there?
Will I suffocate and choke to death, in a tomb that has no air?
Or if I live, and have to lie, all night midst ancient bones,
Breath loathsome smells of rotting flesh, hear shrieks and dreadful moans.

Will all this send me so insane, a bone I'll take from the dead,
And use it as a club to dash, brains out from my head!"

Already it seems I'm seeing ghosts, my cousin is abroad,
He's seeking out my Romeo, who impaled him on his sword.
Dear cousin, wait! Don't fade away, look, see what now I do…
Romeo, Romeo, Romeo…here's drink…I drink to you!"

She drinks the whole vial and falls on her bed.

End of scene 3

Scene 4

Enter the Capulets and the nurse. Capulet speaks.

"Come, stir now all you helpers, the second cock has crowed,
The curfew bell has loudly rung, three on the clock has showed.
Make sure all the food is ready, do not spare the cost,
We've much to do, in such short time, not a minute can be lost."

The nurse implored him, "Go to bed, or tomorrow you'll be ill."
"I've worked all night before," he growled, "never hurt me, never will."
"Look there, below, the bridegroom comes, well dressed for this fine day,
Go wake my daughter, dress her too, go! make haste I say."

The nurse exits.

End of scene 4

Scene 5

The nurse approaches Juliet's bed.

"Mistress, waken, rouse yourself…my lady…please awake.
Oh come now, stir you slugger head, or I'll give you such a shake!
What, not a word, still fast asleep? the curtains I will draw,
Have the morning's brightness light your face, sun through your eyelids pour."

She draws the curtains and sees Juliet on the bed.

"What! dressed in your clothes already, but still asleep in bed?
I must wake you now my lady," *shakes her,* "Oh God!…my lady's…DEAD!
Oh help, my lady's dead," she screamed, "she died whilst in her sleep,
Oh wretched day, so vile, so foul, forever I will weep."

Enter lady Capulet who also starts weeping.

"My child my child, my sweet young life, oh no, this can't be true,
Look up my child, return to life, or I will die with you."
Capulet enters.
"Where's my daughter?" he demanded, "her lord awaits his bride,"
"Oh sir she's dead," the nurse cried loud, "my pretty lamb has died."
Capulet is shattered and inspects the body.

"She does not breath, she's cold and stiff, of life's colour she
has none,
Death lies upon her like a frost, the field's sweetest
flower...gone.
This death that takes her from me, and makes me sob and wail,
Has tied my tongue, I cannot speak, o'er my life has dropped
a veil."

*Friar Lawrence, Paris and musicians enter. Lawrence
speaks.*

"I trust the bride is ready now, to the church, it's time to go?"
"To go there yes," her father wept, "to return...the answer's
'no'.
He speaks to Paris.
The night before your wedding sir, death, with your bride, did
lay,
He wedded and de-flowered her, he's my son-in-law today!"

They wrung their hands in anguish, they moaned in heartfelt
pain.
Cheeks glistened with the tears that fell, they called and called
her name.
"Have done with tears," the friar cried, "though right that you
lament,
There's joy in what has happened...to heaven, she is sent."

"You each had a part in this fair maid, now heaven has her all,
She's better off for in god's hands, there's nowhere she can
fall.
So dry your tears and as custom says, dress her now in fine
array,
Then bear her gently, to the church, a requiem there I'll say."

Capulet, still weeping, gives new orders.

"Things that were planned for the wedding, we must use
another way,

Joyous songs become dark dirges, no instruments will play.
The wedding fare instead will be, served at the funeral feast,
Flowers will now be laid upon, the shroud of our deceased."

The friar called, "Dear brethren, it's time that we moved on,
The heavens soon, will start to frown, if this service is not done.
My lord, go in, and madam too, for this final step…be brave,
Prepare yourselves to follow, this fair corpse unto her grave."

All leave except the musicians brought in for the wedding. Enter Peter, a serving man.

All that were left were musicians, not needed now to play,
They asked Peter what had happened, and would they get their pay.
Peter asked "Pray, play for me, to lighten my dark mood,"
"It's not the time," they told him, "to do so would be rude."

He argued that they play for him, but they would not be swayed,
"Very well," he cried whilst marching out, "I'll make sure you don't get paid."
"He's the kind of knave," one player said, "you never wish to meet,
To hell with him…to the dining hall, and at least get food to eat!"

End of scene 5

End of ACT 4

Act 5

Scene 1

Romeo is awaiting news from Verona and is musing.

"I feel oh so light in spirit, and happy thoughts abound,
I dreamed my lady found me dead, and her kisses brought me round.
Now revived I'm an emperor, she has breathed in me such life,
Balthasar enters
Ah…Balthasar, what news my friend, how is Juliet my wife?"

"And my mother too, my father? pray tell me they are well,
Have you letters from the friar? I'm sure he's much to tell."
"Oh your pardon, sir," said Balthasar, "I bring only news of gloom,
Your wife is dead and as we speak, lies in her family tomb."

"Can this be true?" cried Romeo, "is what you tell me right?
If so find the fastest horses, I must go to her…tonight."
"Have patience sir," begged Balthasar, "your passions now run high,
Remember you are banished, if you're caught sir, you may die."

"I do not care," said Romeo, "just go…do what I ask,
Get the horses then await me, whilst I complete a task.
Balthasar leaves.
If I'm to lie with Juliet, I must find a man I knew,

He trades in deadly poisons, I must get from him a brew!"
He searches the streets.

"I do believe this is the house, I'll call him to the door,
Apothecary…open up, I need something from your store.
Door creaks open
Here's forty ducets, let me have, a poison that's so fast
That he who takes it leaves this earth, as from a cannon blast!"
The apothecary considers for a while and says…

"Such mortal drugs I have sir, but to sell them breaks the law,
To do such a thing could mean my death, but…seeing as I'm poor,
I'll take the risk, accept your gold, and give what you require,
He gives him a vial.
Here, drop this into liquid…drink…you'll quickly then expire!"

"There, take your gold," said Romeo, "but beware it's poison too,
More potent than the drugs you sell, pure evil, through and through.
It was I that sold the poison, you, who sold me none,
Use my gold to put on some flesh, with starving now be done."
Apothecary exits.

"What I hold here isn't poison, but a balm to end my cares, A drink that I will use tonight, and answer all my prayers,
Come with me friend and together ride, to where my lady lies,
Then side by side, we'll rest in peace, 'til your magic, seals my eyes."

End of scene 1

Scene 2

Father John enters with Father Lawrence who speaks.

"Welcome father, have you news? what does young Romeo say?
My letter that you took to him, is his answer here today?"
"I fear not," father John replied, "I still have your letter here,
I could not take it to him, for reasons I'll make clear."

"When I was ready to depart, some townsfolk then fell ill,
I was called to the house infected, my duty to fulfil.
Fearful I could spread disease, some townsfolk sealed the door,
I was locked in till the sickness passed, and the air was clear once more."

"Oh unhappy fortune," Lawrence cried, "my letter he's not read,
Neglecting it could cause great harm, now I must act instead.
Father John go find a crow bar, and bring it to my room,
To save a life I must work fast, pray, bring it to me soon."

Father John exits. Leaving Father Lawrence thinking.

"Alone I must go to Juliet, in three hours she'll awake,
She'll find her Romeo missing, her heart, and mind could break,
Poor living corpse who wakes to find, she's in a dead man's tomb,

'Til Romeo comes I'll hide her, safe and sound within my room."

End of scene 2

Scene 3

Paris and his page are in the graveyard where Paris wishes to spread flowers for Juliet. Paris speaks.

"Give me the torch and when I say, by that tree lie on the ground,
Put an ear to the earth and listen, for the lightest, slightest sound.
If you hear a noise then whistle, it will warn me someone nears,
Do as I say go, take your place, there is no need for fears."

Paris starts spreading flowers on the ground.

Oh Juliet sweet lovely bloom, I spread flowers here for you,
I'll return each night to water them, with tears mixed with the dew. *His page whistles*
The alarm is sounding, someone comes, whose foot roams here tonight?
I'll use the dark to cloak myself, and observe from out of sight."

Enter Romeo and Balthasar carrying tools. Romeo speaks.

"Balthasar take this letter, and at the break of day,
Deliver it to my father's house, do not linger…ride away.
What I do now will concern you, but I charge you on your life,
Do not speak or try to stop me, as I go to my dear wife."

"Give me the tools I'll break in the door, of the tomb where she now lies,
That one last time I'll touch her face, and kiss her shuttered eyes.
Do not return to pry on me, to watch what next I do,
For if you do, I swear my friend, I'll rip your heart in two!"

"I'll go at once," said Balthasar, "and not return to pry."
"I thank you friend," said Romeo, "take this cash, live well...goodbye."
Balthasar leaves, thinking...
"I fear his looks, what he might do, what it is he will not share,
So I'll hide myself and watch and wait, if he needs me...I'll be there."

Romeo starts to break into the tomb, cursing it as he does.

"You detestable gut, you womb of death, fat from the good you've chewed,
I'll force your jaws to open wide, then cram you with more food!"
He set to work upon the door unknowing he was seen,
The count, his page and Balthasar, all watched from in their screen."

"That's the banished haughty Montague," thought Paris as he spied,
"He slew my love's dear cousin, from the grief of which, she died.
It seems he's come to do some harm, to the bodies of the dead,
I'll approach him and demand he stop, and then...I'll have his head."
He steps forwards and speaks.

"Vile Montague stop your evil work, what do you do, and why?
I arrest you and...pass sentence, foul creature, you must die!"
"Indeed I must," said Romeo, "It's why I'm here today,

Tempt me not good gentle youth, pray leave me, go away!"

"I will not," the count cried loudly, "I arrest you for your crime."
"You provoke me," answered Romeo, "draw your sword sir, here is mine."
They start fighting.
"Oh! lord, they fight," the page boy cried, from the shadows of the yard,
"I must try and save my master, I'll run and bring the guard."
The page runs off whilst Romeo and Paris fiercely fight. Paris is mortally wounded.

"I am slain," he sobbed, "I beg you sir, show kindness, hear my plea,
Open up this tomb's great door, with Juliet…there, lay me."
He dies
"In faith I will," thought Romeo, "this man is known to me,
The noble Paris, Mercutio's kin, I'll grant his dying plea."

He opens the tomb door, and enters.

"The dead will now inter the dead, I'll lay him in the tomb,
Then shut the door upon this world, this world of doom and gloom.
He lays the body down then looks around and sees Juliet.
"This is no grave, 'tis a room of light, for here lies Juliet,
She radiates, her beauty glows, she is not conquered yet!"

"Death's pale flag has not advanced, untouched, your beauty's…there!
Your cheeks, your lips, with crimson shine, why are you still so fair?
Does an unknown monster keep you thus, to be his paramour?
For fear of that I'll stay with you, by your side for evermore."

"Here I will take my eternal rest, eyes…look your last on this…

Then arms…take a final warm embrace, and lips…your final kiss."

He embraces and kisses Juliet and takes the poison from his pocket.

"Oh bitter guide, come pilot me, on death's rocks make me fly,

Here's to my love," *(He drinks)* "…oh! this is quick…with that last kiss… I die!"

He dies.

Father Lawrence enters the graveyard and is met by Balthasar. Lawrence greets him.

"My son my greetings, tell me now, what light shines in that tomb?"

"'Tis Romeo's sir," said Balthasar, "it's his torch lights the gloom.

I've not seen what he does in there, for he told me not to stay

But whilst hid I saw him fighting, with a foe that he did slay."

"I must quickly see what's happened, come too," the friar said,

"I dare not sir," said Balthasar, "my lord would have my head!"

"Then stay, I'll go," the friar said, "but fear what I might find,

For the entrance here is steeped in blood, and swords lie on the ground."

He enters and looks around.

"In this palace of peace, now soaked in blood, dead, lies Romeo,

And there nearby him…Paris, and his blood too does flow.

Oh what an unkind sight this is, and what an unkind hour,

For the lady now begins to stir, my draft has lost its power."

Juliet wakes and speaks.

"Good father, tell me, Romeo…is my lord and master here?"
"Let us go from here," he answered, "from this place of death get clear,
For my lady I must tell you, what we planned has all gone wrong,
A greater power intervened…pray hear me and…be strong."

"Your heart, your husband…Romeo, lies there beside you, dead,
And Paris…too lies near you, with death he's also fed.
Come quickly now, don't question me, the guard will be here soon,
I'll hide you in a sisterhood, let us flee this cursed tomb."

"Please go dear father, leave me, I'll stay," wept Juliet,
He leaves.
"I must know what has happened, what death my dearest met.
What's in his hand? why, 'tis a cup, ah…poison caused his end,
And he drank it all, none left for me, not a drop can I call 'friend'."

"Perhaps some still lies on his lips, one kiss is all I need,
As she kisses him, there is a noise outside.
Hark, there's a noise, someone comes, I must quickly do the deed,
His dagger's here, oh happy blade, my heart will be your sheath.
Enter here, stay till you rust, and now…this world, I leave."
She stabs herself and dies.
Enter the page and the guards. The first guard speaks.

"The floor of this tomb is sodden, with blood from all those slain,
Here lies the Count, there Juliet, warm…yet in cold has lain.
Go bring the Prince from the palace, Capulets, Montagues too,

Questions will have to be answered, what tonight here did ensue."
Second guard speaks.

Here is Romeo's serving man, found hidden by the guard,
And here a friar who trembles, caught whilst leaving the yard.
Tools they carried could open graves, crowbars, hammers and saws,
We'll hold them here 'till the Prince comes, he'll know if they've broken laws."

Enter the Prince, attendants, Capulet and lady Capulet. The Prince speaks.

"What misadventure calls us here? why do the people cry?
Some cry Paris, some Romeo, some Juliet…then sigh.
They gather within this graveyard, what is drawing them here?
I dread to think what has happened, certainly nothing of cheer!"

The first guard, pointing at the bodies, speaks.
"Prince, here lies the noble count Paris, there, Romeo…Juliet,
She who was dead now dead again, sad deaths all of them met.
Here is a friar, and Romeo's man, found with tomb robbers' tools,
Tools that could open doors to the dead, tools often used…by ghouls!"

Capulet sees Juliet for the first time and cries out.

"Wife, look how our Juliet bleeds there, sweet blood pours from her chest,
"'Tis a Montague knife protruding, it's sheath now is her breast."
"Oh how this sight tolls like a bell," in tears, his wife replied,

"It warns how life can be shortened, death's call never denied."

Montague arrives and speaks to the Prince.

"Alas my liege, I must report, the death of my wife tonight,
Grief caused by Romeo's exile, took from her the will to fight.
Tell me sir why did you call me? Have I more sorrow to bear?"
"Look and you'll know," the Prince answered, "your son, lying dead…there!"

Montague weeps whilst looking down at Romeo's body.

"What have you done?" Montague cried, "something no father should see,
Your life at its end with you lying, there in a grave before me."
"Hold back your outrage," the Prince said, "'til what caused this is known,
Bring me the two that were captured, to tell why guilt they have shown."

The friar and page are brought in. The friar speaks.

"My Prince you suspect me of murder, no sir, this isn't so,
Hear the sad story I bring you, that truth you will then know.
I married these two lying dead here, God made them husband and wife,
That very same day Tybalt was slain, Romeo…banished for life."

"Juliet pined not for her kin, but the love you had just banned,
Thinking her grief was for Tybalt, marriage to Paris was planned.
She tearfully asked 'could I stop this', if not she said she would die,
I gave her a potion for sleeping, that deathlike she would then lie."

"To her husband I sent a letter, telling what had been done,
That when she awoke he must be there, to take his loved one and run.
Alas, my note did not reach him, rescue then fell to me,
At the hour she woke I got there, aghast at what I did see."

"Paris, Romeo, both lying dead, Juliet holding her man,
Noises we heard, I begged her to come, no, she said, go whilst you can.
I left but it seems she intended to join her lord in death,
All this I swear, and if I hold blame, take sir my dying breath."

"You are still for us someone holy, our friar," the Prince replied,
"Let me hear now from Romeo's man, has he something to hide?"
"I told my lord of Juliet's death, he wept," Balthasar said,
"Then we rode fast to this graveyard, straight to this door he did tread."

"He gave me this note for his father, to hand to him next day,
He threatened my life if I dallied, but I watched as hidden, I lay.
The Prince then turned to the page and asked, "what brought your master here?"
"He wished to spread flowers," he answered, "he did, with many a tear."

As flowers were spread there came a man, trying to batter the door,
My master cried 'stop', drew out his sword...I ran to bring here the law."
"Enough!" said the Prince, "I'm certain now, all that I've heard is true,
Their choice was to die, that after death, their love, they could re-new."

The Prince turns to the feuding parties and admonishes them.

"Capulet, Montague, look there, see what your rivalry's done,
The children you loved, both lying dead, now for your sins you have none.
I too take blame, for I overlooked, too many of your rows,
We've all been punished, now it must end, give me your sacred vows."

Said Capulet to Montague, "will you, sir, give me your hand?
'tis Juliet's gift, for her wedding, no more can I demand."
"I will, indeed," was the answer, "and this I will do too,
In gold I'll coat her a statue, that her name lives after you."

The Prince smiles as they solemnly shake hands. He says…
"A shadowed peace begins to stir, in sorrow hides the sun.
Go hence from here, and talk some more, of the sadness you have wrung,
For there never was a story told with so much tragic woe,
Than this, the tale of two lovers, Juliet, and her Romeo."

FINI

Glossary

'cept	except
e'r	ever
'haps	perhaps
'twas	it was
'til	until
'tis	it is
wil't	will you
Anguish	pain or suffering
Apothecary	chemist
Atone	make amends
Balm	soothing ointment
Bedaubed	covered with dabs of a substance (paint)
Blatant	flagrant, unashamed.
Brash	vulgar, hasty.
Brine	salt water
Chide	scold
Charnel House	house of prostitution
Chastity	virginity
Craw	throat
Contrive	arrange to do something
Decree	official order
Dirges	mournful songs
Distraught	very upset

Doff	lift your hat to someone/give up something
Ducets	gold money
Enmity	hostility
Feud	continuing arguing/fighting between groups over time
Flaunt	show off something
Fraught	filled with danger, tense.
Gory	bloody
Ghouls	someone interested in death, spirit, phantom
Hence	from this time on
Heralds	messengers
Internment	burial
Liege	king
Maskers	people who go to a party in masks
Mortified	feel ashamed.
Paramour	Lover
Palmers	those who carry palm branches
Plight	situation (usually bad)
Provoke	upset someone
Ponder	think about
Portending	warning
Potent	strong
Purged	made clean of

Riles	makes angry
Requiem	mass for the souls of the dead
Scurvy Knave	dishonourable person
Shroud	sheet for putting round a body
Succour	food
Sully	tarnish, disgrace
Truck	dealings
Valour	courage
Vestal	chaste woman
Waxes	increases
Wreak	cause damage.

The Merchant of Venice

The Merchant of Venice was first published in 1600, and thereafter went through a series of revisions which some scholars felt to be badly done, and therefore, misleading. The version in general use today is the one based on the original manuscript of 1600. It is a comedy and like most of Shakespeare's comedies, it is about love and marriage, the path of which is almost always hazardous. It is one of Shakespeare's more disturbing comedies, in that there is much reference to the racism which was prevalent in that age. In this version for young people, this has been reduced to a minimum, and is not specific to any particular race or group. It is hoped that the basic story, as given in this verse form, will be attractive enough to bring the reader back, when older and at an age when racism can be dealt with in an intelligent manner.

Characters in the Play

PORTIA	an heiress of Belmonte.
NERISSA	her waiting gentle woman.
BALTHAZAR	
STEPHANO	servants to Portia.
Prince of MOROCCO	
Prince of ARRAGON	suitors to Portia
ANTONIO	a merchant of Venice
BASSANIO	a Venetian gentleman and suitor to Portia
LEONARDO	servant to Bassanio
SOLANIO	
SALARINO	
GRATIANO	
LORENZO	companions of Antonio and Bassanio
SHYLOCK	a moneylender in Venice
JESSICA	his daughter
TUBAL	another money lender
LANCELET GOBBO	servant to Shylock and later Bassanio
OLD GOBBO	Lancelet's father
SALERIO	a messenger from Venice

The Duke of Venice
Jailer
Magnificoes of Venice Musicians
Attendants and followers

Act 1
Scene 1

Enter Antonio, Salarino and Solanio. Antonio speaks.

"I am so sad, yet know not why, nor from whence my sadness came,
Did I catch it? Was it found? I cannot give it name!
It wearies me, I feel a fool, I do not know myself.
"Your sadness comes," Salarino said," from concerns about…your wealth."

"Your mind is tossing, on the seas, where your merchant ships all sail,
Where misfortune stalks them, every day, 'tis no wonder that you ail.
I too would feel a sadness, to entertain the thought,
Of my ships… so rich in cargo, on rocks, or sand tight caught!"

"Eastern spices, scattered far, silks all soaked in brine,
First… full of worth, then gone like grapes, withered on the vine.
If I were you, with so much to lose, how could I smile… be glad?
Yes, I'm sure it is your merchandise, that makes you feel so sad."

"Believe me, no," Antonio said, "all I have is not afloat,
My ventures are most widely spread, not simply in one boat.

My estate will prosper well this year…should the year be good, or bad,
No, 'tis not my merchandise my friend, that makes me feel so sad."

"Then you're in love," Solanio smiled, but was quickly answered…"no",
"Not in love? Then let us say that this is why you're low,
You're sad because you have no mirth, nothing makes you glad,
But…you could also say you're merry…whenever you're not sad!"

"Like a double-headed Janus, looking left, and also right,
One of nature's oddities, that often come to light.
Like those who look upon strange things, find mirth, then laugh awhile,
Or those whose teeth are never seen, because they cannot smile!"

Enter Bassanio, Lorenzo and Gratiano. Solanio continues.

"But here come friends, we'll leave you now, let's pray they give you cheer,
'till we meet again, when I hope we'll learn, of your sadness you are clear."
They exit.
"Antonio," said Gratiano, "you look worried and not well,
It seems all the world's dark troubles, have you gripped within a spell."

"My dear dear friend," Antonio said, "the world is just…the world,
A stage, where all upon it have, a part to be unfurled.
Mine, alas, is a sad one, that is what you see today."
"Then I'll ease your burden," Gratiano said, "a fool for you I'll play!"

He then began to lecture them, on wrinkles, laughter, mirth,
On his liver, wine, his heart, his groans, but his speech had little worth!
He rambled on and questioned why, some men whose blood was warm,
Would sit just like a tombstone, silent…still…forlorn.

He added, "There are men who think, their silence means they're wise,
That when they open lips to speak, no other voice should rise,
Some are reputed to be sage, because of saying…naught,
But when they do, those that hear, cry…fool…you have no thought!"
He pauses, then…

"For the moment, I must leave you, but, if you're so inclined,
I'll end my exhortation…after diner, when I've dined!"
He and Lorenzo exit.

"Such a windbag," said Bassanio, "and his logic has no shine,
To try to understand his thoughts, is just a waste of time!"

Antonio laughed, and said, "Enough, pray, tell me now the name,
Of the lady, that you hope to wed, whose heart you wish to claim."
"You are aware," Bassanio said, "my estate, alas, is low,
I've not the funds to woo her, so her love for me would grow."

"I have great debts, the most of which, I owe my friend, to you,
In God's good time, I'll honour them, but, must remain now…overdue,
But with lessons learned, I'm wiser, winning ventures will ensue,
Though I owe so much, I ask again, for a loan to see me through."

Antonio answered, "All I have, is unlocked…for you to use,
But tell me first, this plan you have, and just how it cannot lose."
"In Belmonte," said Bassanio, "there's a lady…oh so fair,
When we met, her eyes sent messages…that made me float on air!"

"She has such beauty, and is rich, Portia is her name,
And suitors come, from every coast, her worth now has such fame.
Antonio, had I the means, all rivals I'd make spin,
For the message that her eyes sent, assures me that I'd win."

Antonio smiled and said, "Dear friend, all my wealth is still at sea,
But go to all I trade with, see what my credit here can be.
I too will ask, and know we'll find, a merchant, dealer friend,
Who'll advance you what it is you need, for your venture's fruitful end."

End of scene 1

Scene 2

Enter Portia and Nerissa. Portia speaks.

"Oh Nerissa, I feel weary, this world is tiresome, strange,"
"You would feel so," her maid replied, "if your fortunes were
to change.
Good fortune now, outweighs the bad, you are seated in the
mean,
With neither excess, nor with want...a most happy in-
between."

"Such words of wisdom," Portia said, "that I know I should
pursue,
But, to know what should...or must be done, is easier
than...to do!
This reasoning will never solve, how a husband I can choose,
My father's will states clearly, I can't pick one...nor refuse!"

"Your father," said Nerissa, "had virtuous intent,
He devised a gamble, with three chests, and...this, is what he
meant,
They are made of silver, gold and lead...just one, can a suitor
choose,
He wins whoever picks correct, all other suitors...lose!"

"The one who picks correctly, would bring blessings from
above,
For he who did, would be worthy, good, and you'd marry
him...for love.
So what warmth have you, my lady, for those already come?"

Portia answered, "Give their names...and I'll tell you, one by
one."
Nerissa gives the names...

"The first suitor was Italian, the Neapolitan Prince."
"Ah! Yes," replied her lady, "there's been none quite like him
since!
He could only talk of horses, all else to him was myth,
His dear mother must have dallied, with the local village
smith!"

"Next, was the count of Palatine, a man most nobly bred,"
"But he frowned a lot," said Portia, "a smile would strike him
dead.
I would rather wed a death's-head, with a bone between its
teeth,
Than either of these two so far, they're both beyond belief!"

"Then came Le Bon, the French lord, did he not fit the bill?"
"God made him, on an off day, and he never could sit still.
He would fence his own dark shadow, dance wildly...on a
whim,
I'd have twenty husbands in one man, were I to marry him."

"The English baron...Falconbridge, was he not what you
seek?"
"He'd no Latin, French, Italian...so dumb, we could not
speak!
And how strange his clothing, nothing matched, he knew not
what to wear,
His entire dress, behaviour too, came from...everywhere!"

"Then the Scottish lord, his neighbour, was the next one to
appear,"
"Neighbourly, indeed he was, when...the Englishman boxed
his ear!
For he did not fight, return the blow, but said...'Later!', when
he could!

The Frenchman scoffed at this and said, 'If he didn't…then he would!'"

"The Duke of Saxony's nephew, what made his chances sink?"
"He was vile when he was sober, even viler filled with drink!
At best, he's worse than any man, at worst, more like a beast,
If I had to rate my suitors, I'd rate him as the least!"

"If he chose correct," Nerissa said, "your hand alas, he'd win,
To refuse him, would deny the terms, in the will of your dear kin."
"It will not happen," Portia smiled, "I'd place wine beside the chest,
He'd choose the wine, and God be praised, of a sponge…I'll be divest!"

"Have no fears," her maid replied, "before these lords all left,
They informed me they would not return, of hope they are…bereft."
"I'm glad to hear it," Portia said, "I'll not break my father's will,
Thank God that motley lot have gone, there's not one for whom I'd kill!"

"My lady, can you remember, a soldier, coming here,
Venetian, scholar, handsome…well…in my eyes, did appear?"
"Yes, I do recall," said Portia, "Bassanio was his name,
Most worthy of the praise you give, yes, a man to light a flame!"

Enter a serving man with a message.

"Madam, those who came to woo you, are now ready to depart,
And a messenger awaits with news, of one more who'd have your heart,

A Moroccan Prince approaches, and will be here tonight,
He hopes you'll find him wholesome, as you are, in his sight."

"I feel elated," Portia said, "that my suitors leave today,
If only I could feel the same, now one more is on the way!
Nerissa, come, let's go prepare, for the next depressing bore,
As soon as we shut the gate on one, another's at the door!"

End of scene 2

Scene 3

Enter Bassanio and Shylock. Bassanio speaks.

"I need three thousand ducats, in three months 'twill be repaid,
Antonio is the bondsman, to guarantee this trade."
Said Shylock, "He's a good man, with means profoundly strong,
But… means can be uncertain if…the planning all goes wrong!"

"He has ships upon the oceans, where many dangers lie,
And ships are merely planks and men, through those dangers they must ply.
There are winds, and rocks, and pirates, around them and beyond,
Notwithstanding this, his means are good, and I will accept his bond."

"To be quite sure, I'd speak with him, to talk details of our deal,"
"Of course," replied Bassanio, "will you take with us a meal?"
"I think not," answered Shylock, "you use foods I must not eat,
I'll walk with you, buy and sell with you, but to dine? …we cannot meet!"

Enter Antonio whom Bassanio introduces to Shylock, Shylock thinks to himself…
"I dislike this lordly, pompous man, his business ways I hate,
He loans out money free of charge, then I must drop my rate!

101

He scorns my people, rants and raves, complains of what I charge,
He calls it…'interest', I say…it's thrift, contempt for him grows large!"

Bassanio nudges Shylock who was deep in thought He excuses himself with…

"I was counting all the funds I have, and find I'm slightly short,
But, I'll borrow from a friend of mine, whose assistance can be bought."
"I borrow not," Antonio said, "and neither will I lend,
But, to meet the needs of my dear friend, my rule, this time, I'll bend."

Shylock tells a story to try and justify his methods.

"In the Bible, there's a story, of interest," Shylock said,
"It will help you understand it, and of interest…lose your dread.
An ancestor called Jacob said, he'd guard his uncle's sheep,
Through the many months of winter, 'till lambs began to leap'."

"For payment he agreed to take, those born with coloured wool,
'Impossible!' his uncle thought, 'my nephew is a fool.'
But Jacob was an artful boy, and devised a clever trick,
Before each ewe about to lamb, he placed colours on a stick."

"The ewes saw colours, every day, and when lambing time began,
Many coloured, baby lambs were born, fulfilling Jacob's plan.
This was his interest, he was blessed, perhaps now you'll understand,
Interest is, a blessing sir, not something underhand."

"Your Jacob," said Antonio, "could not do a thing...so grand,
He had no gift, so, it must have been, with heaven's helping
hand."
He laughed, and said to Shylock "Tell me if you would,
Was not this story used to make, your 'interest' look good?"

Aside he says to Bassanio...

"This devil can cite scriptures, to serve his dubious ends,
He's evil using holy words, his smooth villainy...offends.
But alas, we need what he can give, though we'll be in his
debt,
So Shylock, can we now agree, the terms that we must set?"

"You've berated me," said Shylock, "many times in the
market square,
You've condemned the way I bargain, think my methods
crude, unfair,
You called me once a cutthroat cur, and spat upon my cloak,
Yet now it seems, you want my help, I'm no longer just a
joke!"

"Yes spat on me, and cursed my name, kicked me like a dog,
Should I forget such courtesies, come fawning...all agog!
Should I approach with bated breath, say...sir, on me you
spat,
But here's a loan sir, take it, please, bend low and doff my
hat?"
"I'd likely say it all again...and spit!" Antonio said,
"If you are to loan me money, keep these words within your
head,
Regard me as your enemy, that should I so default,
You can then impose the penalty, with clear, untroubled
thought!"

Shylock said, "I heed your words, and this we must do now,
Go together to a notary, and seal with me this vow.
That...should you not repay me, at the place and date agreed,

The borrowed sum...and interest, with this fine...I can proceed."

"From your body...at my choosing, a pound of flesh be cut,
Should this be done, I will declare, the book on this deal...shut."
"This is fair," Antonio said, "to these terms I do agree."
"No!" cried out Bassanio, "you'll not agree to this for me!"

"Be not afraid," Antonio said, "I'll not have to pay the fine,
A month before the bond expires, my fortunes start to shine!"
Shylock waited whilst they talked, thinking to himself,
"What happens if he does default? ...it adds not to my wealth."

"Man's flesh is really worth much less, than mutton, beef or goat,
'Tis not for gain my offer's made, I'd hardly earn a groat!
It is to buy his favour, with friendship then in view,
I hope he will accept it...if not...I'll say...adieu!"

"To the notary then," Antonio said, "where this bond I'll sign and seal,"
"And whilst you do," said Shylock, "I'll get ducats for the deal.
Presently, I'll meet you there, with the ducats in my purse,
I too will add my signature, and the money then disburse."

Shylock exits

Said Antonio, "How friendly, it shows, he can be...kind."
"I don't like his terms," said Bassanio, "nor his evil, crafty, mind!"
"Be of cheer," Antonio smiled, "there's no reason for dismay,
My ships return with all their wealth, one month, before the day."

They exit

End of scene 3
End of ACT 1

Act 2
Scene 1

Enter the Prince of Morocco, a tawny-coloured Moor with attendants. Also Portia, Nerissa and attendants. The prince speaks.

"Dislike me not for my colour, 'tis work of the sun above,
Here where the sun just melts the ice, I've come to offer my love,
This hue on my face, frightens foes, attracts young maidens too,
I'd never wish to change it but…would if it helped win you."

Portia replied, "I have told you, my fate depends on a chest,
Pure chance will bring me a husband, not the heart that beats in my breast.
This was the wish of my father, on free choice, he placed a bar,
Had he not dear Prince, your chance is as fair, as any I've seen so far."

"For that," said the Prince, "I thank you, lead on where the caskets lie,
I'll make my choice, the moment of truth, when love, will live, or die.
I'd outbrave rivals, fight wild beasts, if that, would win your hand,
But this! …is just the throw of dice, blind fortune…nothing planned."

"You must take your chance," said Portia, "but swear now, 'fore you do,
Should wrongly you choose, speak not of love, or come here again to woo."
"I swear it so," the Prince answered, "I will not return again,
So, to my fate, shall I be blessed, or fatally cursed amongst, men?"

They exit
End of scene 1

Scene 2

Enter Lancelet Gobbo the Clown. He is also Shylock's manservant, and is thinking of leaving his employ.

"Should I run away from my master, my conscience tells me...no!
But my bad fiend within says leave him, leave him...run away...go!
Again, the fiend says leave him, go get your things and pack,
My conscience replies with...no sir!... Go put those things, right back!"

"My conscience says I am honest, being an honest man's son,
Well...perhaps not man, but woman, strange things, my father has done!
Budge, budge not...budge, budge not, my conscience and fiend can't agree,
But I like best my fiend's advice, I'll take it...yes, I will flee!"

Enter Lancelet's father, old Gobbo, who has poor eyesight. He speaks,

"Would'st show me the way to Shylock's house, my eyes can't properly see?"
Lancelet thought, "Oh, dear heavens, my father knows not it's me.
Turn left, then right," he directed," left, then right once again."
"Gracious!" cried Gobbo, "I'll not find that, instead I'll give you a name,"

"Lancelet…lives he with Shylock? Is it yes sir, or is it no?"
Lancelet answered by teasing, "To heaven I'm told he did go!"
"Oh, mercy," cried Gobbo, "I'm saddened, he was my staff and my prop."
"Do I look like a prop?" his son answered, "this foolishness now has to stop."

"Father, do you not know me?", "No," his father replied
Lancelet kneels before him
"Well now old man, listen to me, I'm your son, and I haven't died!"
Said Gobbo, "Please do not kneel sir, I'm sure you're not my son,"
"Father, I am…your boy, your child…with nonsense let us be done!"

"Margery was my mother's name…the same as that of your wife."
"It is," cried Gobbo, "now I believe, you ARE, that prop of my life,
But oh how you've changed…your beard so long, more than the tail on my horse,
And how is Shylock, your master? I've brought him a present of course."

Lancelet answered, "He starves me, I'm thinking of leaving his house,
I wish to work for Bassanio, not that loathsome old louse.
So father give *him* that present, help me to gain his employ,
he looks along the road
What luck! …Bassanio comes here, let's hope my day ends in joy."

Enter Bassanio, Leonardo and a few friends

"God bless your worship," said Gobbo…"and you," was the warm reply,

"Is there something you wish to ask me, the reason, I caught your eye?"

Gobbo replied, "'tis my son sir, a poor but honest young boy,
He toils and slaves for Shylock, but wants to leave his employ."

"No sir not poor," cried Lancelet, "I work as a rich man's man,
But he treats me wrong, I must leave him…and then, serve you…if I can."

"Shylock has told me," Bassanio said, "he'd not object, if you,
Were to leave the riches of his house, for mine that has so few!"

"The proverb goes," said Lancelet, "The Grace of God is enough,
You have the grace, he has enough, my choice sir, isn't so tough!"

Bassanio smiled, "Well spoken, to Shylock's …go say goodbye,
Come later this day to my house, a uniform there to try."

Bassanio turns to speak to others whilst Lancelet speaks to his father.

"So, let us go now to Shylock's, and there bid that foul man…farewell,
My fortune now will be brighter, the lines on my palm so foretell."

They exit and Gratiano enters.

"Bassanio," called Gratiano, "a favour of you I would ask,
May I go to Belmonte with you, for there dear sir, I've a task?"

"If that is your wish," Bassanio smiled, "so it shall be, my friend,
But hear my words, so we ensure, the friendship we have doesn't, end.

You, have high spirits, can be quite rude, wild, in things that you say,
We know you well…others do not, offence, they could take away."

"So should you join me, I must insist, on modesty, manners, from you,
Those, where we go, I must impress…so your company don't let me rue!"
"Pray hear me sir," said Gratiano, "I vow that whilst we're away,
I'll wear sober habits, curse and I'll swear only a little each day!"

"Prayer books I'll have in my pocket, and often, I'll say…Amen.
I'll be civil, well mannered, respectful, and ever polite to all men."
Bassanio laughed, "Pray not tonight, be bold my friend with your fun,
Tonight when we dine we need laughter, without you, there would be none!"

End of scene 2

Scene 3

Enter Shylock's daughter Jessica and Lancelet Gobbo (the clown) Jessica speaks.

"I'm sorry that you are leaving…this house is often like hell!
To me you were sometimes a devil, bringing much fun to its shell.
A guest is at your new master's, Lorenzo is his fair name,
Please give him this note in secret…if seen, it could bring us shame."

"Adieu sweet lady," said Lancelet, "my tongue is tied by my tears,
I'll pass on your note as asked me…dear lady, please have no fears."
He exits.
"Farewell good Lancelet," she answered, "God speed you on your way,
Deliver my letter soon there, let nothing cause you delay."

"What heinous sin lies inside me, that I should feel such shame,
To be my father's daughter, that I share, his blood, and name!
Lorenzo, please keep your promise, take me away from this strife,

That I become a good Christian, and then, your loving wife."

End of scene 3

Scene 4

Enter Gratiano, Lorenzo, Salarino and Solanio talking about the feast at Bassanio's

They talked of masks they'd be using, at Bassanio's feast that night,
Of wearing fine fancy clothing, of torches bringing them light,
Lancelet enters.
And as they talked, Lancelet pressed, the note in Lorenzo's hand,
He read it and smiled on learning, what his true love had planned.

Lancelet speaks to him.

"My master sends me," Lancelet said, "to bid Shylock here to dine,
I could take with me your answer, the pleasure sir, all would be mine."
"You are most kind," said Lorenzo, "when you can, with Jessica share,
This happy message I send her…fear not, for I will be there."

Lancelet exits followed by Salarino and Solanio, still talking about the feast. Lorenzo speaks to Gratiano.

"Gratiano, I must tell you all…tonight, I shall elope,
Fair Jessica will flee with me, we are filled with love, and hope,
With jewels and gold and finery, she waits at her father's house,

I'll take her from his evil grasp, that she becomes my spouse."

They exit

End of scene 4

Scene 5

Enter Shylock and his former servant Lancelet. Shylock speaks.

"Your eyes shall judge the difference, 'tween Bassanio and me,
You'll not eat as well, or feel the warmth, that this house gave to thee!
Jessica enters,
Ah Jessica, I've been asked to dine, at Bassanio's tonight,
I don't know why, they love me not, I've no standing in their sight."

"I sense such ill will towards me, I'm really loathe to go."
"But you must go sir," cried Lancelet, "my new master wants it so,
The diners will all wear fancy dress, fun masks to hide their face."
"Such revelry ends," said Shylock, "in drunken, vile, disgrace!"

"So daughter...lock my house up and should rowdiness draw near,
Venture not upon the streets, stay safe, and sound, in here.
I've no mind for feasting out tonight, but Lancelet, get thee hence,
Tell your new master I'll be there, though against, my better sense!"
Before he leaves, Lancelet whispers in Jessica's ear,

"Mistress, when the moon shines above, keep a sharp watchful eye,
For this message I bring…a young man will come by!"
He exits, Shylock speaks.
"I thank the lord," said Shylock, "he no longer works for me,
To feed him cost a fortune, and what he did here's hard to see."

"I've passed him on to my debtor, he's paid from a borrowed purse,
'twill help to waste, the borrowed sum…and the debt to me grow worse."
He exits.
"Farewell father," Jessica thought, "if my fortune is not crossed,
For me…'twill be a father, and for you…a daughter lost!"

End of scene 5

Scene 6

Salarino and Gratiano are waiting outside Shylock's house for Lorenzo, to help him to elope with Jessica. They question the wisdom of what he is to do. Gratiano speaks.

"Lorenzo aims to elope tonight, to seal his lover's bond,
He showed such spirit for the chase, but, does he see beyond?
Who rises from a sumptuous feast, with the hunger that he sat?
What horse that races outwards fast, can race with the same speed back."

Lorenzo arrives and greets them.

"I thank you dear friends for waiting I'm so sorry that I'm late,
Should ever you go, thieving for wives, if needed *I'll* stand and wait!"
This house is the house of Shylock, look at that window above,
Sweet Jessica there awaits me, she who has won all my love."

Softly she called, "Catch this casket, within, is all I possess,
I'm glad it is night for you cannot see, the way that I've had to dress,
I blush at the thought that to leave here, I must disguise as a boy."
"No matter my love," said Lorenzo, "however you look gives me joy!"

"The night slips away, come down at once, betrothal for us awaits,"
"I'll first get more ducats," she answered, "then close and lock all the gates."
She disappears.
Whilst waiting Lorenzo spoke warmly, of changes to come in his life,
Then she came to his side and whispered… "Come now, make me your wife."
The all leave, except Gratiano who is joined by Antonio who speaks.

"There'll be no feast tonight my friend, the wind's now strong and fair,
Bassanio goes to board his ship, and asks that you join him there,"
"I'm glad," replied Gratiano, "and filled with such delight,
I'll join him now, that we may be, in sail and gone tonight."

The exit
End of scene 6

Scene 7

Enter Portia with the Prince of Morocco and attendants. A curtain is drawn back to reveal the three caskets.

"You may now make your choice," said Portia, "of gold, silver or lead,
You'll win if you choose the box that holds, a portrait of my head.
If so you choose, I will be yours, forever dear Prince and a day,
So take your pick, throw down your dice, hoping it falls your way!"

The Prince studies the boxes and notices an inscription on each. He reads them aloud.

> *"GOLD: who chooseth me shall gain what many men desire.*
> *SIL VER: who chooseth me shall get as much as he deserves.*
> *LEAD: who chooseth me must give and hazard all he has."*

The Prince thinks about this trying to make a judgement He thinks aloud.

"Says this box of lead if you choose me, you must give, and risk, your all,

Give all for what? Risk all for lead? My int'rest in lead starts to fall!
This box is a threat, I'll not take risks, without hope of fair return,
It has the look of worthlessness, I think, this box, I'll spurn!"

"If silver I choose it says that I'll get as much as I deserve,
That has to mean the sweet lady...she that I'm longing to serve,
I deserve her by birth and by graces, also my long pedigree,
Should I stop now? Choose right here? Or, consider, box number three?"

"Casket three is the box of gold, 'twill give what men desire,
Why, again it must be the lady, the one, that I so admire.
Not only me but other men too, have journeyed, both far and wide
Crossing high mountains, deserts and seas, hoping she'll be their bride."

"Her image now lies, in one of just three, surely it cannot be lead!
The thought is so base, who'd put it there? Is it then, silver instead?"
But, silver's worth is less than gold's, a fool must clearly see,
Gold is the setting for a gem such as she...YES! ...GOLD...pray give me the key!"

Portia gives him the gold key...he opens the box, and gasps!

"There's a skull within!" he cried aloud, "each eye is an empty hole,
Protruding from one there seems to be, writing on a wound scroll."

He reads it aloud.

> *"All that glitters, is not gold,*
> *Often have you heard that told.*
> *Many a man, his life hath sold*
> *But my outside to behold.*
> *Gilded tombs do worms infold,*
> *Had you been as wise as bold,*
> *Young in limbs, in judgement old,*
> *Your answer has not been inscrolled,*
> *Fare you well, your suit, is cold.*

Cold indeed, I have wasted my chance, Portia…alas, I have lost,
I feel too aggrieved to make sad farewells, my dice was wrongly tossed!"

They all exit
End of scene 7

Scene 8

Salarino and Solanio are talking about the robbery of Shylock. Solanio speaks.

"The Duke has been asked by Shylock, to help find what he has lost,
Golden ducats…precious stones, such an enormous cost!
They went to search Bassanio's boat, he had sailed, as the wind was keen,
But later that night escaping, the thieving pair, were seen."

"I've never heard such passion, rage, Shylock seemed…confused,
Whilst in the street he was shouting, 'I'm robbed, I've been abused!'
He bewailed his loss of ducats, his jewels, and so much more,
He commanded that his child be caught, and brought, before, the law!"

"He ranted like a madman, creating quite a scene,
If his fortune's not recovered, I fear he could get mean,
Friend Antonio should heed this, and be sure to meet the date,
For if he can't, our friend may meet, a nasty, bloody, fate!"

Salarino told then what he'd heard, from a sailor yesterday,
"An Italian ship off England sank, and now on the seabed lay,
It was richly laden so I fear, belonged to Antonio,
If it does alas, that debt looms large, and can only give him woe!"

"When Bassanio left Antonio said, think not about the debt,
Only think of what you must do, to win she, you've gone to get,
Do not hurry your return, stay long, if needs you must,
Think not of me my dearest friend, you wil! always have, my trust."

They exit to join Antonio to give him comfort if necessary.
End of Scene 8

Scene 9

Enter Portia, Nerissa and the Prince of Arragon. *The boxes were explained to him.*

Another suitor came to call, the Prince of Arragon,
He knew he had to choose correct, for Portia, to be won,
He read each casket, one by one, dismissing lead outright,
He turned then to the other two, their metals shining bright.

Gold he thought too showy, glittery and slick,
A gaudy box would be the thing, the common man would pick!
So gold too was rejected, leaving silver as his choice,
"Give me the key to this one," said he in his haughty voice.

He opens the silver casket and pulls out a scroll and a portrait. He looks at it and gasps.

"This portrait is not Portia, 'tis of a stupid fool!
I assumed that I, deserved the best, but a fool's head?…this is cruel.
Is this my prize? Can this be all? What else has this box in store?
This writing here, upon the scroll, perhaps will tell me more."

He reads aloud.

> *"The fire seven times tried this;*
> *Seven times tried that judgement is*
> *That did never choose amiss.*
> *Some that be that shadows kiss;*
> *Such have but a shadow's bliss.*
> *There be fools alive, iwis,*
> *Silvered over – and so was this.*
> *Take what wife you will to bed,*
> *I will ever be your head,*
> *So be gone; you are sped."*

The Prince continues

"Still more fool I shall appear
By the time I linger here.
With one fool's head I came to woo,
But, I go away with two.
Sweet adieu, I'll keep my oath,
Patiently, to bear my wroth."

He exits.

Enter a messenger who speaks to Portia.

"My lady, waiting now outside the gate, is a young Venetian man,
He precedes his lord and asks that he, speak with you, if he can,
An ambassador of love I think, to prepare you for his lord,
As well as greetings he brings gifts, which he hopes you will applaud."

"Bassanio!" cried Nerissa, "let us hope that it is he,
That Cupid can then do his work, and Bassanio so win thee."
Laughed Portia, "You so praise this man, I wonder...is he kin?

125

No matter…I'll see for myself…Nerissa bring him in!"

End of scene 9
End of ACT 2

Act 3
Scene 1

Enter Salarino and Solanio talking about Antonio's ships at sea, Salarino speaks.

"It's rumoured yet another ship floundered and then sank,
Richly laden, lost at sea, on a fatal sandy bank.
Let's pray this is the end of it, he'll suffer no more loss,
But wait! Here comes the devil…Shylock…looking cross!"

Shylock enters, Solanio greets him.

"How now Shylock, bring you news? What do the merchants say?"
"The talk is of my daughter sir, the one who flew away.
My flesh and blood, a rebel…I damn and curse her soul,
It makes my poor heart flutter sir, to think of what she stole!"

Said Salarino, "Ah! Your daughter, your flesh, your blood…and yet,
You are more unlike each other, than is ivory and jet!
But Shylock, please, enough of this, tell us what you know,
Has Antonio lost another ship?…is it yes, or is it no?"

"I did badly there," cried Shylock, "he, who was so smug
Now a bankrupt, beggar too, slinking like a slug!
He hardly dares to show his head, he's truly had his day,
Let him look now to his bond, I intend to make him pay!"

"If he forfeits," Salarino said, "surely you'll not press
To use the law, enforce the bond, and take your pound of
flesh?"
"The flesh," said Shylock, "I would use, as bait for feeding
fish,
If nothing else I'd have revenge, and fulfil a long held wish!"

"This man abused me, many times, laughed at my losses…my
gains,
Scorned my people, thwarted my deals…causing such
heartfelt pains,
He's heated my foes, cooled off my friends, why does he do
such things?
I'm not of his race or religion…from that…his enmity
springs."

"Have I not eyes? Have I not hands? Organs, passion and
heart?
Do I not eat? Fall ill, be healed? If slapped, do I not smart?
If I am pricked, do I not bleed? If tickled, do I not squirm?
If I am poisoned, would I not die, like him, lie feeding the
worms?"

"If we are wronged, should we not fight? as you have taught
us to do,
That which you taught us, we will improve, it will go harder
for you!"
A messenger enters and speaks to Salarino and Solanio
"My master the lord Antonio, is at his home today,
I'm sent to ask that you join him, to hear what he has to say."
They exit.

Enter Tubal. Shylock speaks to him.

"How now, Tubal, have you news? Is my errant daughter
found?"
"I've searched far and wide," said Tubal, "with neither sight
nor sound,"

"The thief's gone with so much," wailed Shylock, "with much spent to find that thief,
Oh, were she dead, my gold returned, I would not suffer such grief!"

"But other men too," said Tubal, "have also had bad luck,
Antonio's ship from Tripoli, sank when lightning struck."
"Oh! wondrous news," cried Shylock, "good news, good news indeed,
If only for the briefest while, I'm distracted from my seed!"

"In a single night," said Tubal, "your daughter, so I've heard,
Spent more than fourscore ducats, such spending is absurd."
Shylock wept, "'tis a dagger sir, that you've just thrust in me,
Fourscore ducats! …in just one night! …that's gold I'll never see!"

"Antonio," Tubal continued, "most certainly is undone,
His Venetian creditors say now, bankruptcy soon must come."
Said Shylock, "True, so get thee hence, find me a man of law,
I will drive this man from Venice, that I may take the floor!"

They exit
End of scene 1

Scene 2

*Enter Bassanio, Portia, Gratiano, Nerissa and their
attendants. They have come so that Bassanio can make his
choice of casket. Portia speaks to him.*

"Soon you'll have to make your choice, if wrong, you'll have
to go,
So pause a while before you do, that each other, we may
know,
Oh! If I could, I'd keep you here, for months before you
choose,
I'd teach you how to do it right, to ensure you do not lose!"

"But, alas I cannot do it, 'tis against my father's will,
Even though a wrong choice means, our love we'll not fulfil.
We are barred from what, should be our right, but none will
hear our voice,
I speak too long, on purpose for, it delays your fateful
choice!"

Bassanio cried, "Forgive me, I can no longer wait,
I feel I'm being tortured when, I do not know my fate.
So lead me to the caskets now, that one I can select,
If right I choose, my life begins, if wrong, my life lies
wrecked!"

"Then go," said Portia, "make your pick, as you do let music
sound,
It will softly fade if you choose wrong, in my tears you'll then
be drowned.
If you win, the music rises, as at the crowning of a king,

It will summon you to marriage, a church, a bride, a ring!"

Bassanio goes to the caskets and stands considering them.
As he does, the music starts, in the form of a song.

> *Tell me where is fancy bred*
> *In the heart, or in the head?*
> *How begot, how nourished?*
> > *Reply, reply.*
> *It is engendered in the eye,*
> *With gazing fed, and fancy dies*
> *In the cradle where it lies,*
> *Let us all ring fancy's knell,*
> *I'll begin it – ding, dong, bell*
> *Ding, dong, bell*

Bassanio thought both deep and long, on what each box could mean,
And finally determined things…are not quite as they seem.
"Ornament is but what it is, decoration, nothing more,
This gaudy gold is Midas food, I dismiss the golden ore!"

"The silver also I'll dismiss, 'tis in such common use,
But you my poor, and meagre lead, what in you do I deduce?
You threaten, yet you promise nought, this moves me to the quick,
Here I choose, let joy abound, yes, lead…will be my pick."

Portia is overjoyed because she knows he has made the right choice.
He reaches in and takes out her portrait, and a scroll

"Behold! The portrait, I have won, fair Portia do I see,
'tis beautiful, but a shadow of, the reality…of she.
How could an artist capture all, her lips, her eyes, her soul?
But I have done so, by my choice, now, let me read the scroll."

131

You that choose not by the view
Chance as fair and choose as true,
Since this fortune falls to you,
Be content and seek no new,
If you be well pleased with this
And hold your fortune for your bliss
Turn you where your lady is,
And claim her with a loving kiss.

"A gentle scroll fair lady, I almost can believe,
It has given me permission, to give and to receive,
But, never quite, I'm full of doubt, how can all this...be true?
Until confirmed and ratified, signed and sealed by you."

"My lord Bassanio," Portia said, "here starts my wondrous dream,
I'll devout my life, do what I must, to stand high in your esteem,
In life I am unpractised, but young enough to learn,
I commit myself to you my lord, all others I do spurn!"

"Myself, this mansion, all within, I now convert to you,
Where once I ruled and ran this house, it's now for you to do.
My gentle spirit waits command, by my governor and king,
All that I have is yours now, I seal it with this ring."

"But if ever you misplace it, lose, or give it away,
'twill signify the loss of love, that your feet were made of clay!"
"Were this ring not on this finger, here's why," Bassanio said,
"Life will have left my body, Bassanio would be dead!"

Gratiano and Nerissa heard, all that had been said,
Smiling, they then both announced, they too, would like to wed!
Said Gratiano, "When you made your pick, I admit, my mouth was dry,
For not only was your fate at stake, mine too was riding high!"

"To me, this maid had vowed her love, if her mistress you did win,
My lord you have, let me win too, that both our lives begin."
"If this is true," smiled Portia, "with joy I give consent."
"As do I," Bassanio added, "if this is your intent."

"We are honoured in your marriage, that you too will be as one,
And a thousand ducats wager, on who first begets a son!
But here's my friend Lorenzo, with Jessica his bride,
And another friend, Salerio, what brings you to our side?"

He introduces them to Portia who welcomes them. Salerio hands Bassanio a letter from Antonio. Bassanio reads it and Portia reacts to the expression on Bassanio's face.

"There is something in that letter, drawing colour from your face,
A dear friend dead? A relative? What is it you embrace?
My lord, I am now half of you, if this note has brought you pain,
We must share the pain together, or nothing shall we gain."

"Oh sweet Portia," Bassanio cried, "these words are so unkind,
A letter that could hurt me more, would be difficult to find,
When first I brought my love to you, I said I'd little wealth,
That what I had ran in my veins, my manners, breeding, health."
"I fear I was a braggart, with less than what I said,
For I borrowed through my dearest friend, to pursue that we be wed,
The ventures he embarked on, now appear to all be lost,
And the man he owes great debts to, demands he pays the cost."

"Salerio friend, is this all true? Have all his ventures failed?
Not one bit from around the world, every ship of his that sailed?"
"Not one my lord," Salerio said, "and even if it had,
Shylock would refuse plain cash, his behaviour's gone…quite mad!"

"Both day and night, he plies the Duke, for what he calls his right,
He threatens to impeach the state, for justice he will fight.
The Duke and many good men too, have begged he drop his claim,
But to enforce the bond and get his flesh, is now his only aim."

Said Jessica, "When in his house, I overheard him swear,
He'd rather have Antonio's flesh, for the money…he'd no care!
If the law does not deny him, the powers tell him…NO!
I'm afraid my lord, it will go hard, for poor Antonio."

"Is he so dear," asked Portia, "that you tremble at his plight?"
"Most dear, and kind," he answered, "and most noble in my sight,
He owes three thousand ducats, all due to my account."
"Is that all he owes?" cried Portia, "he's to die for that amount?"

"Pay him double, treble…even more, and have this bond defaced,
The friend you describe is priceless, and should never be disgraced,
First my love, we'll marry, then to Venice…save your friend,
We'll pay that petty debt tenfold, the guilt you bear must end."

"And when it's paid bring your good friend here, to rest a while and heal,
But 'fore you go…to our wedding where, our promises we'll seal.

We ladies here, will await you, like widows we shall be!
First though read Antonio's note, that I share what so moved thee."

He reads the letter aloud:

"Sweet Bassanio, my ships have all miscarried, my creditors grow cruel, my estate is very low, my bond to Shylock is forfeit, and since in paying it, it is impossible I should live, all debts are cleared between you and I. If I might but see you at my death. Notwithstanding, use your pleasure. If your love does not persuade you to come, let not my letter."

"Such love!" cried Portia, "go now, go, do what needs be done."
"I'll make haste," Bassanio answered, "embrace you and be gone,
'till I return there'll be no bed, to be guilty of my stay,
Let nothing come between us, be true…whilst I am away."

They exit
End of scene 2

Scene 3

Enter Shylock, Solanio, Antonio and his jailer. Antonio speaks.

"Good Shylock, stay and hear me, pray pause and let me speak,"
"I will not pause," said Shylock, "I know what you would seek,
Without just cause, you called me dog, so now beware my teeth!
I'll have my bond you may not speak, no more you'll cause me grief!"

"I'll not be made a dull-eyed fool, to sigh, relent, then yield,
You may not speak, I'll have my bond, on that I am quite steeled."
He exits.
"Such a wretched man," Solanio said, "vile unto his core."
"Let him be," Antonio sighed, "I'll plead with him no more!"
"He seeks my life with reason too, 'oft times I've caused him pain,
I've used my skills, to make him lose, that I could make a gain,

He'll have his bond, it is the law, on that our state depends,
Bassanio's debt I will repay, then I care not if life ends."
Antonio is taken away by his jailor.
End of scene 3

Scene 4

Enter Portia, Nerissa, Lorenzo, Jessica and Balthazar, Portia's manservant. Lorenzo speaks.

"He who you send relief to now, is a noble gentleman,
And has loved your lord and husband, since their boyhood first began."
"From what I've heard," smiled Portia, "together they are...whole,
By saving one, I save the two, and therefore save my soul."

"Lorenzo. I have made a vow, that until my lord's return,
I'll live within a monastery, the outside world I'll spurn.
Nerissa will go with me, to await her husband too,
Can I leave the cares and running, of this household all to you?"

"With all my heart," Lorenzo said, "I'm honoured that you ask,
And whilst away have peace of mind, I gladly do this task."
He and Jessica exit.
"Now Balthazar," said Portia, "you must help me with my plans,
With speed take this note to Padua, place it in my cousin's hands."

"He will give you notes and robes, bring them quickly back to me,
At the Venice ferry landing, I'll be waiting there for thee."
Balthazar exits with the note.
"Nerissa come, we've work to do, of which you're unaware,

137

We will go to where our husbands are, in a way to make them…stare!"

"For we will dress as smart young men! and swagger round the town,
I'll brag about my conquests, with a voice that I'll keep down!
I'll turn mincing steps to manly strides, wear a dagger with brave grace,
I'll boast of how the ladies swoon, when I merely show my face!"

"But why must we go," Nerissa asked, "disguised in young men's dress?"
"Please, no questions," Portia said, "as time begins to press.
I'll explain all that I'm planning, later in our coach,
For we must measure twenty miles, before the night's approach."

They exit
End of scene 4

Scene 5

Enter Lancelet, the clown, and Jessica. Lancelet speaks.
"It is sad for you that a father's sins, are laid upon his child,
You are damned alas, but with some hope…albeit rather wild!
If your father's not your father, of his sins then you are free."
"Then my mother's sins," said Jessica, "will be those that fall
on me!"

"Then truly you are damned by both," laughing, he replied,
"I worry not," she answered, "for I am my husband's bride.
I share his faith and thinking, now my father's I disown,
I'll suffer not damnation, salvation I've been shown."

Lorenzo enters.

The clown in Lancelet played his role, he amused them with
his fun,
'til Lorenzo, laughing cried "Enough! with bantering…we're
done.
Go tell the staff prepare our food, select for us a wine,
Come Jessica, my wife my love, it's time for us to dine."

They exit.
End of Scene 5

End of ACT 3

Act 4
Scene 1

Enter The Duke, Venice Magnificoes, Antonio, Bassanio Salerio and Gratiano. The Duke speaks.

"Antonio I'm so sorry, I've done everything I can,
You must answer your adversary, a vile and wretched man.
He shows not a drop of mercy, of pity…even less,
His loathing of you is so deep, he'll take nothing but your flesh!"

"I thank Your Grace," Antonio said, "that you tried to intercede,
But he's obdurate and rigorous, determined to proceed.
There's no lawful way to carry me, beyond his envy's reach,
I will not beg and plead with him, my honour I would breach."

Shylock enters and the Duke speaks to him.

"Shylock, I and all the world believe, your malice is an act,
That now the time to pay has come, you'll show mercy love and tact,
You'll abandon your demand for flesh, and the penalty disown,
And touched by humane gentleness, forgive some of the loan!"

"Be it known, sir," answered Shylock, "by the Sabbath, I have sworn,
I'll have the forfeit of my bond, from that, I'll not be torn.
If you deny it, danger falls, upon your City Charter,

I swear that through the law I'll break, it's right to trade and barter."

"You ask...why flesh not money? Here's how I answer that,
Should I not spend to rid my house, of a loathsome little rat?
I trust you are now answered, if not then hear this too,
I hate this man Antonio, so my forfeit, I'll pursue!"

Bassanio pleaded further till, Antonio cried, "No more,
You may as well tell the tide...'go back'...whilst standing on the shore.
Make no more offers to this man, it's time to pay the bill,
Let me have my judgement now, and Shylock have his will."

The Duke to Shylock turned and said, "Mercy...you've shown none,
How can you, sir, expect it, should your time for mercy come?"
"Why should I need it?" Shylock said, "I've not done any wrong,
I stand for judgement, give it now, my case is fair and strong."

"This case will be judged," the Duke announced, "by a doctor of the law,
I've asked that he come here today, and from me take the floor.
Bellario is this doctor's name, a wise and learned man,
He will determine rights and wrongs, and submit to us his plan."

Nerissa enters, disguised as Bellario's clerk. She gives the Duke a letter which he reads. Meanwhile, Shylock starts to sharpen his knife on the sole of his boot. Bassanio speaks to him.

"Why whet your knife so keenly, what do you hope to gain?"
"That bankrupt's flesh," cried Shylock, "he'll not trouble me again."

"You make it keen," Gratiano said, "but never will it be...
Half as sharp as the malice, that pours from the soul of thee!"

"Are there no prayers to pierce your heart, to make it melt or break?"
"None," said Shylock, "that you have, the wit, or sense, to make!
Save what you have, you silly youth, your pleading I deride,
There is nothing further to be said, the law is on my side."

The Duke has read the letter and makes another announcement.

"This letter from Bellario, commends another to our court,
He too is a learned doctor, in the law most highly taught."
"He awaits outside," Nerissa said, "for Your Grace to call him in."
"Then call him now," the Duke replied, "so this hearing can begin."

Whilst awaiting the doctor, the Duke reads the letter to all assembled.

"Your Grace shall understand that, at the receipt of your letter, I am very sick, but in the instant that your messenger came, I was being visited by a young doctor of Rome. His name is Balthazar. I acquainted him with the cause of the controversy between Shylock the money lender and Antonio the merchant. We turned over many books together. He is furnished with my opinion, which, bettered with his own learning (the greatness of which I cannot commend enough) which comes with him at my importunity to fill up your Grace's request in my stead. I beseech you let his lack of years be no impediment to him giving a reverend estimation, for I never knew so young a body with so old a head. I leave him to your generous acceptance."

Enter Portia disguised as the lawyer Balthazar.
"Ah, here's the doctor," smiled the Duke, "and welcome, take your place,
Are you aware what separates, the parties in this case?"
"Indeed I am sir," Portia said, "but know not who is who,
Who is the money lender here, and who is overdue?"

Each was introduced to her, and judgement then began,
"Venetian law," said Portia, "for the plaintiff strongly ran,
Perhaps because it is so strong, some mercy you should show."
"For what reason," Shylock asked her, "should mercy I bestow?"

Portia answers…

> *"The quality of mercy is not strained,*
> *It droppeth as the gentle rain from heaven*
> *Upon the place beneath. It is twice blest:*
> *It blesseth him that gives and him that takes.*
> *It is an attribute to God Himself:*
> *And earthly power doth then show like God's*
> *When mercy seasons justice. Therefore, Shylock,*
> *Though justice be thy plea, consider this:*
> *That in the course of justice none of us*
> *Should see salvation. We do pray for mercy,*
> *And that same prayer doth teach us all to render*
> *The deeds of mercy."*

"I hear your plea," said Shylock, "and take note of all you've said,
But still demand that the law be served, let blame fall on my head."
"The money then," said Portia, "could that not be repaid?"
"I have it here," Bassanio cried, "more! …if it closed the trade!"

"Twice the sum I'll pay this man, and if that will not suffice,

I'll bond myself ten times more, if that, would break his ice!
I'll stand in forfeit of my life, but if this won't void his bill…
I beg your Grace to use the law, to curb this devil's will."

"It cannot be," said Portia, "there's no power in the land,
A decree, once written, is the law, the State can't countermand."
"Oh wise young judge," smiled Shylock, "I truly honour thee,"
"Pass me the bond," said Portia, "there's something I must see."

She reads the bond and speaks.

"Why, this bond is forfeit, so by law, your claim you can now press,
From near the heart you may cut, a pound of this man's flesh,
But Shylock, pray, show mercy, of law be not so fond,
Take trice the money, even more, let me tear up this foul bond."

"You're a worthy judge," said Shylock, "you know well Venetian Law,
I demand that you now use it, and justice thus ensure.
There's no power in the tongue of man, to make me change my mind,
I'll take now the flesh as stated, in the bond that this man signed!"

"So be it then," said Portia, "merchant…bear your breast,
Prepare yourself, for Shylock's knife, to plunge into your chest."
"Oh noble judge," smiled Shylock, "such an excellent young man,
Much older than the years you show, your wisdom serves my plan."

"Are your scales all ready," Portia asked, "to weigh your pound of flesh?"
"They are, indeed," said Shylock, "one pound, no more, no less,"
"And your surgeon too," she asked him, "that from bleeding he'll not die?"
"No such clause in the bond," he said, "I saw no reason why."

"It does not matter," Portia said, "now…what says Antonio?"
"I'm well prepared," he answered, "for whatever fate may throw.
Farewell my good Bassanio, and the love we've shared so long,
Commend me to your lovely wife, and grieve not when I'm gone."

"Oh, my friend," Bassanio cried, "my wife, my life, my all,
I would sacrifice most gladly, if it saved you from this fall."
"You'd get no thanks," said Portia, "if your wife were here today,
To hear the offer, you just made, to give everything away!"

"I too love my wife," Gratiano said, "but would wish her in God's care,
If there she had the power to lock, this monster in his lair!"
"It is just as well," Nerissa said, "that was said behind her back,
For I fear if known, within your house, peace you'd sadly, lack!"

"We trifle time," said Shylock, "I pray thee let us start."
"The court agrees," was the answer, "One pound, from near his heart."
"Most learned judge," said Shylock, "come let us now prepare."
"A moment," Portia told him, "of this are you aware?"

"The bond does not allow you blood, just a simple pound of flesh,
So have your bond, but ere you do, there's something I must stress.
If in cutting this man's breast, one drop of blood is shed,
Your lands, your goods, are confiscate, as the law falls on your head!"

"Is that the law?" frowned Shylock, she answered, "read the Act,
You ask for justice…that, you'll get, and more…'twill be a fact!"
"Then I'll take the offer," Shylock moaned, "thrice the sum, I'm owed,
Release the merchant, let him go, there!…mercy, I have showed!"

"Wait!" she ordered, "you shall have, just that, which you demand,
His flesh is what you asked for, that's all you can command.
So prepare yourself to cut away, shed not a drop of blood,
A pound…not a hair's weight more or less, or upon you…falls a flood!"

Shylock hesitates

"Why do you pause?" asked Portia, "judgement has been given,
Take now the flesh, the forfeiture, for which you were so driven."
"I've changed my mind," said Shylock, "give my loan back then I'll go."
"I have it here," Bassanio cried, but Portia ordered, "No!"

"Many times you've turned cash down, sir, here, in open court,
All you're left with now to claim, is the forfeit you have sought."

146

"Can I not just have my principal?" Shylock meekly said,
"Only the forfeit," she replied, "at your peril if he's bled!"

"The devil take it!" Shylock cried, "I'll not be questioned more,
I'll stay no longer in this court, I'm done with your foul law!"
He starts to exit.
"I say tarry there," said Portia, "there's a further hold on you,
When you resolved to take his flesh...you bit too much to chew!"

"The law here states if an alien, of which sir, you are one,
Seeks the life of a citizen, harsh sanctions must be done.
Half he owns the victim takes, the other half, the State,
The offender's life is forfeit but...the Duke can mitigate."

"You contrived to take this merchant's life, mercy...you'd not give,
So down before the Duke I say, and beg he'll let you live."
"I grant you mercy," said the Duke, "and this before you plea!
'twill show the spirit of our State, the gulf 'tween you and me."

"Half you own goes to Antonio, the other, to the State,
In another act of humbleness, the State's half...I'll abate."
"You have my home," sobbed Shylock, "and all else I had to give,
You may as well, sir, take my life, I've no reason now to live."

Portia asked Antonio, "what mercy would you show?"
"If it please the court," he answered, "adjust the judgement so,
The State's share be reduced by half, this then goes to me,
That on his death I pass it on, to his daughter, forced to flee."

"For the favour you have shown him, I ask for two things more,
He shall become a Christian, and this shall be the law.

On his death all he possesses, all he's earned, or all he's won,
Be gifted to his daughter, and to Lorenzo, now his son."

"This he will do!" declared the Duke, "or else I shall withdraw
The pardon that I gave him, all mercy shown before."
"What say you Shylock?" Portia asked, "with this are you
content?"
"I am content," he murmured, "with disputing I am spent!"

"Clerk, now prepare a deed of gift, for signing," Portia said,
"Pray…let me leave here," Shylock moaned, "I feel a sickness
spread,
Have the deed of gift sent to me, I'll sign it when I'm rest."
"Be sure you do," the Duke said, "or of life you'll be divest!"

Shylock exits. The Duke speaks to Portia.

"Please, join me at my house to dine, it would give me much
delight."
"Your Grace," said Portia, "pardon me, I must away tonight."
"Then Antonio," the Duke said, "It's for you to thank this
man,
To express our deepest gratitude, for his wise and learned
plan."
The Duke exits.

"Most worthy, sir," Bassanio said, "my friend and I, you
freed,
Wilt take these ducats that were meant, for sating Shylock's
greed?"
Antonio added, "Noble sir, of this, you can be sure,
For what you've done you'll have our love, and service,
evermore."

"He is well paid," smiled Portia, "who is well satisfied,
In saving you, I'm satisfied…well-paid can't be denied!"
"Then dear sir," Bassanio said, "I must try once again,
To offer you a token that, will bring to you my name."

"You press me hard," said Portia, "pray, let me see your hand,
I'll take that ring, you're wearing, yes! I'll have that little band!
Do not draw back, I'll not take more, is what I ask...amiss?"
"This trifling thing?" he answered, "I'd be shamed to give you this."

"I want nothing else but this," she said, "there! I've set my mind."
"I'll find you another ring," he cried, "of the more expensive kind!
For this was given by my wife, and this vow to her I made,
I'll not give, nor sell, nor lose it, from this vow...I'll not be swayed!"

"That's just an excuse that men use, to not give gifts," she said,
"Your wife would forgive you if she knew, I saved your good friend's head!
She'd think me most deserving but...if still your answer's...nay,
I'll return myself to Padua...and bid you all...good day!"

She and Nerissa exit whilst Antonio speaks to Bassanio.

"Bassanio, pray, give him your ring, he has so earned our love,
He was sent for our deliverance, as if, from God above.
Your wife will forgive for she will hear, the debt that we both owe,
Let Gratiano overtake him, with the ring our love bestow."

Bassanio agrees and sends Gratiano, with the ring, to catch up Portia.
Bassanio and Antonio exit to get ready to leave for Belmonte the next day.

End of scene 1

149

Scene 2

*Portia and Nerissa, still in disguise, on their way to
Shylock's house, are caught up by Gratiano with the ring.
Portia is speaking to Nerissa.*

"We must find the house of Shylock, and take to him this
deed,
To ratify our agreement, his signature we need.
Then tonight we'll take these guises off, to Belmonte we'll
away,
To get there before our husbands, we cannot stay to play!"

Gratiano arrives and speaks to them.

"On more advice, my noble lord, sends me here to give this
ring,
And with it too his warm invite, to dine with him I bring."
"I gladly accept the gift," she said, "but alas, I cannot dine,
But please show this youth to Shylock's house, this document
there to sign."

"I know it well," he answered, "This way, sir, if you please."
To Portia, Nerissa whispered, "My husband now…I'll tease!
I gave him a ring when we were wed, to keep it he did swear,
I'll ask him now to give it me, as a token I can wear!"

"If you do persuade him," Portia said, "there'll be much
swearing…when,
They plead and try to convince us, they gave their rings…to
men!

We'll ask how could they do this, whilst we were being chaste?
But this is all for when we're home, Nerissa go, make haste."

End of scene 2
End of ACT 4

Act 5
Scene 1

Enter Jessica and Lorenzo.

Jessica and Lorenzo stood together 'neath the moon,
They marvelled how, on such a night, their love began to bloom,
And on such a night each lost their heart, and the other's they had won,
And on such a night from Venice ran, to start new lives, as one.

Enter Stephano, a messenger from Portia.

"I bring word to you, my mistress comes, before the break of day,
She pauses first at the holy cross, there to kneel and pray.
I ask you sir is my master here, from Venice now returned?"
"Not yet," replied Lorenzo, "of his passage we've not learned."

"But as the mistress of this house, will soon be with us here,
You and I, sweet Jessica, must prepare the house with cheer."
Enter Lancelet, with a letter.
"There's a post come from my master, it says he's on his way,
He'll be with us ere the morning, when dawn begins the day."

Lancelet exits, Lorenzo speaks.

"We must fill the house with music, have music fill the air,
Stephano, bring musicians here, we'll have music
everywhere.
Let sweetness touch your lady's ear, let sweetness draw her
home,
We'll make her feel so welcome that…no more she'll wish to
roam."

"Sweet music always makes me sad," said his lady with a
sigh,
"The reason is," he answered, "it makes spirits want to fly!
The man that has no music, nor is moved by music sounds,
Is only fit for savage deeds, his coarseness knows no bounds."

"Whatever forms his spirit, is dull and black as night,
His emotions lie 'tween earth and hell, and rarely see the light.
Let no such man be trusted, such a man is incomplete,
Ah! No more talk, the music starts, let's pause and the
music…greet."

*Enter Portia and Nerissa. They hear the music and Portia
speaks.*

"Nerissa, listen, music, so much sweeter in the night,
If heard by day, 'midst other sounds, 'tis drowned and put to
flight.
Ah, here's Lorenzo, welcoming. Sir…are our husbands
home?"
"No, not as yet, my lady, but their coming is now known."

"A post has told us they'll be here, before the break of day."
"Make sure," she answered, "the staff don't tell that we have
been away!"
A trumpet sounds
"Your husband is at hand," he said, "his trumpet I did hear,
Fear not my lady, none will tell, about your absence here."

Enter Bassanio, Antonio, Gratiano and their followers.

Portia welcomed her husband home, and too, Antonio,
Gratiano greeted Nerissa, and love again did flow.
But soon an angry voice arose, a quarrel did ensue,
"Whatever is it?" Portia cried, "what is between you two?"

Gratiano cried, "'tis about a hoop, a paltry ring of gold,
That she did give me when we wed, that I've neither lost
…nor sold.
I gave it to the judge's clerk, a youth, a well-scrubbed boy,
By the moon above she does me wrong, to say with love I
toy!"

"When I gave it," said Nerissa, "to keep it you did swear,
I'll make sure this clerk, who has it now, on the face will grow
no hair!"
"He will if he lives, to be a man," curtly, he replied,
"If a woman lives to be a man, perhaps she would," she
sighed!
"You are to blame," said Portia, "I must be plain with you,
To part so slightly with her gift…when no longer in her view.
You have caused your wife unkind grief, to break your vow
is sad,
If the ring I gave my love were lost…I confess, I would be
mad!"
Bassanio swallowed hard and thought, "I'd best cut off my
hand,
And swear I lost it fighting, defending her sweet band?"
"My lord Bassanio gave his too, to the judge," Gratiano said,
"The judge demanded only that, he'd take nothing in its
stead."

"Alas, neither man nor master, would vary his demand,
We fought, but then unwillingly, we bowed to their
command."
"What ring did you give him?" Portia asked, "pray…not the
one from me."

"The ring is gone," he admitted, "I will not lie to thee."

"You made a vow, but your heart was false, by heavens," Portia said,
"Until I see that ring again, I'll not come to your bed!"
"Nor I to yours," said Nerissa, "'til I again see mine,
'Til then my erring husband, you will have to bide your time!"

"Sweet Portia," cried Bassanio, "I pray you hear me now,
Understand then feel the pain I felt, when forced to break my vow.
If you knew how this judge had saved us, you'd know…I had no choice,
You would soften condemnation, and take harshness from your voice."

"For me, the ring's symbolic," she said, "with meanings you should know,
If you'd thought of honour, promise, you would not have let it go.
You defended it so poorly, without fervour, zeal or sting,
I'll bet my life it is a fact, a woman has that ring!"

"By my soul and honour, that's not true," hotly, he replied,
"Not a woman but a doctor, who refused all else I tried.
He had saved the life of my dear friend, what else then could I do?
If you'd been there my dear lady, you'd have begged I give it too!"

"Let not that doctor," Portia said, "anywhere near my home,
He has the jewel you swore to keep, so like yours my favours…roam,
I'll not deny him anything…yes…the body that you wed,
Watch over me for if you don't, I'll have him in my bed!"

Nerissa added her part, saying, "As will I…his clerk,
So be advised protect me…from your duty do not shirk."

"If he comes near," Gratiano growled, "he'll leave unhappy when…
I take him roughly to one side, and break the young clerk's pen!"

"Stop this now," Antonio cried, "It's me that is to blame!"
"Grieve you not," said Portia, "you are welcome just the same."
"Oh Portia!" sobbed Bassanio, "forgive that I have erred,
Forgive and by my soul I'll swear, no more to break my word."

"For your husband once," Antonio said, "I gladly pledged my life,
I dare be bound again today, unto Bassanio's wife,
I put my soul as forfeit that the vow that you just heard,
Will not be broken by your lord, no more he'll break his word."

"Then you shall be his surety," smiling, Portia said,
"Give him this ring and bid him thus, with this one, keep your head!"
"It's the same I gave the doctor," said Bassanio with a cry.
She answered, "The doctor gave it, when with him I did lie!"

"Gratiano," said Nerissa, "here's a ring that you must see,
For this, that boy, the doctor's clerk, last night did lie with me!"
"Are we cuckolds?" Gratiano raged, "a title…undeserved."
"Speak not so grossly," Portia urged, "for the truth will now be served!"

She gives them a paper.

"This, is from Bellario, explaining all our work,
I, Portia, was the doctor…Nerissa there, my clerk.
Lorenzo is our witness, he saw us on our way,
And Antonio here's a letter, good news for you today."

"There you will find three of your ships, have richly come ashore,
I think from now your solvency, will trouble you no more."
Antonio cried, "I am amazed, struck dumb, I cannot speak,
I am given back my living, my life's no longer bleak."

"The doctor! ...YOU!" Bassanio cried, "I really did not know,
You shall be my bed mate doctor, to my wife's bed you may go!"
"And YOU! his clerk," Gratiano laughed, "who's face will grow no hair,
Unless you grow to be a man...when a little may grow there!"

"My clerk," smiled Portia, "brings good news, for Lorenzo and his wife,
They inherit all rich Shylock owns, at the ending of his life...
'Tis almost morn, the night is done, so let us now withdraw,
We'll go inside for comfort where you may question us some more."

"Before we do," Gratiano said, "I shall ask my newlywed,
With the night near done my dearest, do we stay, or go to bed?
When the day peeps through it will be light, I'll be wishing it were dark,
For then is the time when I, at last, will lie, with the doctor's clerk."

FINI

Glossary

Agog	expectant
Aggrieved	being upset, having a grievance
Adieu	goodbye in French
Albeit	though be it
Abate	Reduce
Bereft	deprived of
Berated	told off
Bated breath	anxiously
Braggart	someone who boasts
Confiscate	take away
Chaste	abstaining from sex
Cuckolds	the husband of an adulteress
Dubious	doubtful
Ducats	old time's money
Deferred	make concessions/ postponed
Exhortations	urgings
Enmity	hostility
Errant	deviating from
Forlorn	sad and lonely
Fiend	evil spirit
Forfeit	surrendered as a penalty
Groat	old times money
Gilded	gold leaf
Gaudy	flashy in appearance
Heinous	horrible
Haughty	Haughty
Intercede	intervene on behalf of
Janus	a mythical god
Jet	pitch black (stone)
Mean	average (in the middle)

Misconstrue	arrive at the wrong meaning
Midas	a god who turned things to gold
Meagre	very little
Malice	ill feeling toward someone
Mitigate	lessen/ reduce
Obdurate	hardened against
Plaintiff	a person bringing a law case
Principal	the original sum in a loan
Revelry	fun and games (usually with drink)
Ratified	confirmed (usually in writing)
Rigorous	strict/ severe
Sage	wise
Spouse	a married person
Sumptuous	lavish
Sating	gratify to the full
Solvency	having enough money to meet needs
Unfurled	Opened
Ventures	undertakings (sometimes risky)
Virtuous	possessing morals
Whence	from where
Whet	sharpen